OPERATION
Pucker Up

Rachele Alpine

ALADDIN M!X

New York   London   Toronto   Sydney   New Delhi

This book is a work of fiction. Any references to historical events,
real people, or real places are used fictitiously. Other names, characters,
places, and events are products of the author's imagination, and
any resemblance to actual events or places or persons,
living or dead, is entirely coincidental.

ALADDIN M!X
Simon & Schuster Children's Publishing Division
1230 Avenue of the Americas, New York, NY 10020
First Aladdin M!X edition July 2015
Text copyright © 2015 by Rachele Alpine
Cover illustration copyright © 2015 by Frank Montagna
Also available in an Aladdin hardcover edition.
All rights reserved, including the right of reproduction in
whole or in part in any form.
ALADDIN is a trademark of Simon & Schuster, Inc.,
and related logo is a registered trademark of Simon & Schuster, Inc.
ALADDIN M!X and related logo are registered
trademarks of Simon & Schuster, Inc.
For information about special discounts for bulk purchases,
please contact Simon & Schuster Special Sales at 1-866-506-1949
or business@simonandschuster.com.
The Simon & Schuster Speakers Bureau can bring authors to your live event.
For more information or to book an event contact the
Simon & Schuster Speakers Bureau at 1-866-248-3049
or visit our website at www.simonspeakers.com.
Cover designed by Karin Paprocki
Interior designed by Mike Rosamilia
The text of this book was set in ITC Berkeley Oldstyle.
Manufactured in the United States of America 0615 OFF
2 4 6 8 10 9 7 5 3 1
Library of Congress Control Number 2014946260
ISBN 978-1-4814-3236-8 (hc)
ISBN 978-1-4814-3235-1 (pbk)
ISBN 978-1-4814-3237-5 (eBook)

To the Beck Center for the Arts . . .
my childhood home away from home

CHAPTER One

IT'S PRETTY MUCH IMPOSSIBLE TO GET out of Mrs. Reichard's room during one of her history lectures. Many have tried, but few are able to claim success.

All my other teachers let you go to the bathroom if it's an emergency, but Mrs. Reichard is not like most teachers. She acts as if leaving her class is a personal attack on her. The woman drones on and on and absolutely refuses to let anyone get up and leave until she's done "filling your heads with my wondrous fountains of knowledge," as she says. Short of needing serious medical attention, you're stuck in her room until the bell rings. Actually, I'm not even sure calling 911 would work.

But today I had a mission. And I wasn't about to let anything stop me. Not even Mrs. Reichard and her "fountains of knowledge," because class was over in ten minutes and I needed to see the cast list for *Snow White* before anyone else.

I raised my hand as she babbled on about the settlement of the American West. She paused and lifted her eyebrows as if I were interrupting the most thrilling discussion ever (which, for your information, it was not. Not even remotely close. It looked as if half the class were trying to stay awake, and there was one kid in the corner who had lost the battle and was drooling onto his desk).

"Yes, Grace?" She peered at me over the top of her bright red reading glasses and looked positively peeved that I had the nerve to disturb her lesson.

"Can I go to the bathroom?" I wiggled around a little bit, hoping she'd get the idea of how important the situation really was.

But of course she didn't buy it.

"How about you wait until class is over," she said in a way that was not a question, but what my English teacher called an imperative sentence.

"I can't. This is an *emergency*," I told her, and squirmed even more in my seat to make it seem like this was a life-

or-death situation. Some of the kids around me giggled. My face flushed red, but it didn't matter. Let them laugh. I needed to complete this very important task, and time was not on my side.

"I don't see any reason why you can't hold it for the ten more minutes we have left in class." Mrs. Reichard turned her back to me and wrote some notes on the board.

"Please," I begged, even though this was getting downright humiliating. I imagined my classmates whispering in the hallway about how close I came to having an accident in history. They'd point and laugh and make up some awful nickname that had to do with diapers or something equally embarrassing.

She sighed so loud, I swear it shook the walls. "Go ahead, but hurry back."

"Thank you, thank you, thank you!" I shouted, and jumped up. I glanced at my best friend, Lizzie, as I raced to the door. She rolled her eyes, and I winked at her. She knew I was going to see if the list was posted. It always went up at some point during last period, right before the school day was over. Probably because our director, Mrs. Hiser, didn't want to deal with the drama from those who didn't get the parts they wanted. Mrs. Hiser was smart. Post it when everyone was leaving and our parents would be the first ones forced to listen to us complain, not her.

I learned the hard way how important it is to look at the list alone. Last year I thought I was going to get a lead role and talked about it the whole day. I checked the list with the rest of my friends only to discover I was cast as Snowflake Number Three. I wasn't even Snowflake Number One. The experience taught me that it's a lot easier to find out you got a teeny-tiny part when there aren't a whole bunch of people around you.

I rushed out of the room but slowed down to check and make sure the hall monitors weren't around. If they spotted you anywhere but the bathroom, it was back to class immediately, and I couldn't risk getting caught before I completed my mission. I used my ninja-like skills and moved through the hallway undetected.

Finally, I made it to the last hallway before the drama wing. As soon as I turned the corner, I instantly knew the scene I caused in class was worth it, because the list was up! The bright yellow paper hung in the center of the bulletin board. The palms of my hands started to sweat and my heart pounded. I approached slowly, and when I stood in front of it, I put my hand in my pocket and pulled out my lucky marble. I closed my fingers around it and squeezed tight before I looked at the list.

Now, I'm not a superstitious person. I stroll under ladders as if it's no big deal, open umbrellas inside because it beats getting rained on when you have to do it outside, and if a black cat crosses my path, I'll bend down to pet it.

I don't believe in any of that ridiculous stuff. Nope. Not at all.

Until I audition for a play.

Then I turn into a person obsessed with the power of lucky charms, because ever since I discovered my magical marble, I've been cast in every show. Mom says I get the parts because I'm talented, and she might be right—and I've taken many acting, dancing, and singing classes—but I firmly believe that if I didn't have my marble, I'd be doomed to a life of stage crew. Not that there is anything wrong with stage crew, but why would I want to hide behind the curtain when I could be out front where I belonged, blinded by the bright lights shining on me?

I clutched my marble, closed my eyes, made a wish, and read the names from the bottom of the list to the top like I always do. It helps prolong the seconds I can imagine I might still have a chance at the lead. Sometimes the anticipation is better than the actual real thing, especially when the real thing means getting a part like Snowflake Number Three.

My eyes moved higher and higher, and I held my breath, hoping against hope I was Snow White. *Please let me get the part, please let me get the part*, I chanted to myself.

My friends Lizzie, Beck, and I had sat together in the theater watching each person audition, and they both pinkie-swore I was the best Snow White out of the whole bunch. I didn't say anything back to them, but I silently agreed. I rocked the audition. Usually I'm nervous before trying out, but not that day. I walked across the stage and said my monologue as if I had been born to play the Fairest in the Land. And now the time had come to see if all my hard work had paid off.

I found Beck's name and giggled when I saw he was Grumpy the Dwarf. Beck was the complete opposite of grumpy; I don't know if I have ever seen him in a bad mood. He would get to show off his acting chops with that role. Lizzie was on the list too, as a townsperson, which would make her happy. Lizzie was more of a small-role type of girl. I, on the other hand, most certainly was not.

I rolled the marble around and around in the palm of my hand as slowly, slowly, my eyes made their way to the top, and there, right at the very tippy-top, was my name.

Grace Shaw: Snow White

Me! Me! Me!

I couldn't help it. I threw my hands up in the air and danced. I totally busted it out in the middle of the hallway. A hall monitor stared at me, so I waved, because, really, what did it matter? I didn't care at this point if the whole school saw me breaking it down. It wasn't every day that a seventh grader got the lead in Sloane Middle School's play. Usually those parts were given to eighth graders, but not this time!

I looked at my name again and touched it. My fingers traced the letters, and I fist-pumped the air.

This was big! This was major! This was the best day of my life!

CHAPTER
Two

I WANTED TO WAIT UNTIL DINNER TO tell Mom and my little sister, Claire, about my part. My news was worthy of a celebration and it was Friday Pizza Night. All kinds of wonderful things happen on Friday Pizza Night. It was next to impossible to keep my mouth shut when I got home, but somehow I managed it. Even when Mom asked me how my day at school was, I shrugged, pointed at my book bag, mumbled something about having homework, and ran upstairs.

I lay on my bed for the next hour as the light outside faded and it grew dark. I imagined telling Mom and Claire I was going to be Snow White. Mom would get a big grin on her face and probably run over and hug me in her super-tight, embarrassing way so that even if I wanted her to let go, she wouldn't. Claire would start to giggle and get excited, because *Snow White* is one of her favorite movies.

But that never happened, because when I got downstairs, my whole world came to a screeching halt.

Dad was at the dinner table.

"Hi, honey," he said, sitting in the seat he hadn't sat in for months. Nine months, three weeks, and one day ago, if you want to be specific. I could probably figure out the minutes and the hours, too. Because the thing is, there's no way you could forget what time of day it was when your parents told you they were going forward with a "trial separation," a decision Dad said was best for everyone, even though we all knew it was only best for him.

I froze, and for a moment I thought I was seeing things. What was going on? Dad hadn't been home for months and now suddenly he was at our kitchen table? I pinched myself to make sure this was real, because it didn't make any sense, but sure enough, I felt it, which proved that he really was sitting there.

"Hi?" I responded, the word sounding more like a question because I felt like I was dreaming. Dad was the last person I expected to find when I came down to dinner, and I wasn't prepared for this.

I glanced at Mom and Claire and they both seemed perfectly fine with having Dad here, which didn't make any sense at all. None of this made sense.

I pulled my chair out slowly to avoid making the awful scraping sound Mom hated. I sat down and stared at the purple nail polish chipping off my fingers in order to avoid looking at Dad.

I couldn't believe he was sitting at our table for Friday Pizza Night.

This was the only time Mom allowed us to have food that wasn't low cal, no fat, organic, packed full of nutrients, free range, or any of those other crazy health-nut terms she always threw around. The type of food that caused me to pick broccoli out of my teeth and wish for a big greasy hamburger when I was done eating it. Mom had been on this health kick since Dad walked out. She said it was about time we all started to watch what we ate, but I think it was just something for her to use as a distraction.

Tonight Dad sat in the seat that was once his. The one with the view of the TV in the family room so he could see the game during dinner.

Operation Pucker Up

My stomach sank when I realized why Dad was here. My parents must be making a divorce official. It was obvious this was their way of "breaking the news gently" and telling us together, so one of them didn't appear to be the bad guy, even though Dad pretty much claimed that role when he got his own apartment.

But Mom didn't act like something was wrong with this picture. She had followed our usual Friday Pizza Night routine and changed out of her work clothes into jeans and a big comfy sweatshirt, and pulled her black hair into a ponytail. She placed the pizza boxes on the table with a stack of napkins, because one of the rules was that when we ate pizza, we didn't have to worry about plates or place mats or anything polite. We ate straight from the box and pulled long ropes of cheese off the gooiest pieces, plopping them right into our mouths.

Mom sat down with us. Everyone reached for slices and chowed down as if this were a normal Friday night. The three of them talked and joked like what was happening wasn't totally unusual. Mom finished her crust first, like she always did, and Dad joked with Claire about some field trip her third-grade class went on. Even our Scottish terrier, Darby, seemed to welcome Dad. He stayed right next to Dad's chair and wagged his tail every time Dad looked his way. I couldn't make myself feel the same, though, because I knew he wasn't here for anything good. He was just going to hurt us again, so before Claire could get too comfortable with him, I decided to say something.

"What are you doing here?" I asked.

Mom said I was famous for being blunt. I blurted things out all the time before stopping to think whether they were polite or not. Once I asked the lady across the street when her baby was due only to find out she wasn't pregnant. Yeah, not cool. My defense to Mom was my inquisitive mind, but tonight I was fine with being straight-out blunt.

"Grace," Mom said in the voice she used when Claire and I fought. The voice that meant, *Stop it right now and act like the big sister or you'll be in trouble.*

Dad finished chomping his pizza and focused on me. "I know I haven't eaten dinner with you girls in a long time, but things are going to change. Your mom and I have been talking for a while now, and we're happy to say things are going well between us."

I studied my parents, confused. Things were going well between Mom and Dad? Since when? Had they been secretly seeing each other? I kept my mouth shut, because how do you respond to something like that?

I didn't like the sound of this "well." I raised an eyebrow at Dad. "Well" was a suspicious word. It was what you told your parents when they asked how you did on a test and you didn't want to admit you bombed it. "Well" was what you said when your grandma was sick but you weren't supposed to tell people she was sick.

I glanced at Mom to see what she thought, but before I could figure it out, Dad reached out and touched the top of my hand. "We thought it would be good if I moved back in."

"Yay!" Claire shouted at the same time I pulled my hand away.

If someone had asked me to list all the reasons Dad was in our house tonight, moving back in would not have been one of them. Dad wanting to return home didn't make sense. On Mom's sad days, she'd snuggle with Claire and me on the couch under a pile of blankets and tell us about how happy she was that it was the three of us. She called us the Terrific Three, girl power prevailing as if we were a trio of superheroes.

I thought about the way tonight was supposed to go. When I'd daydreamed earlier about sharing my big news, this was not what I'd pictured. Now was definitely not the time to tell everyone about getting the role of Snow White. Especially after Dad dropped this bomb on Claire and me. How could I compete with something like that?

Things got super quiet and awkward. I picked at the cheese that was getting all rubbery on my pizza and thought about where Dad was living since he moved out—an apartment fifteen minutes away. Claire and I spent every other Saturday with him. That was the deal my parents agreed on, even though they hadn't asked me how I felt about it all. I dreaded those Saturdays, because it felt like we didn't fit into Dad's life. Claire and I never stayed over; instead, we got lunch at this little restaurant by Dad's place and then sat around his tiny apartment, where the only cool thing was the building's indoor pool. But even that wasn't so great, because once I went down to swim and found Band-Aids floating on the surface.

"This is a good thing," Mom said, finally speaking. "We're a family; we need to be back together."

"We sure do," Claire said. "Now we can go to the zoo, and the water park, and you can come to my school for our Halloween party." Claire rambled on about all the great things she planned to do with Dad now that he was back.

"Those sound like great ideas, sweetie," Dad said.

Claire continued to chew her pizza with her mouth open,

Mom acted as if this was any other Friday Pizza Night, and Dad sat there in his chair as if it was right where he belonged.

All I could do was think about the last play I was in. Only two weeks after my parents separated, Dad missed the spring musical. Mom told Claire and me over and over again that their problems were between the two of them, but when Dad didn't turn up to my show, it proved she wasn't telling the whole truth. He wasn't taking a break from Mom, but from all of us. So now that he was back in the house, how could I celebrate the lead in the play without remembering how Dad had reacted to my last one?

"This is going to be a change," Mom said. "But it's good. It's so good for us."

"Your mom is right. It's time I come back home," Dad said.

"You're going to leave again," I said quietly. I still missed Dad like crazy. I'd spent months wishing he would come back, but it didn't matter. If he left us once, he'd leave us again.

"Grace—" Mom started, but Dad interrupted.

"It's okay. This is a lot to take in. It's going to be an adjustment."

Tears welled up in my eyes. How had things gone so wrong? I wasn't supposed to make Mom mad and yell at Dad. We should have been laughing and joking and celebrating my big part in the play. That's what tonight was supposed to be about.

"May I be excused?" I asked before I completely lost it. I didn't wait for anyone to give me permission. I left. I didn't even look at Mom, because I was afraid of what I might see. It hurt that she was willing to let Dad move back in so easily. None of this was okay, and now I was forced to sit in my room alone and try to figure out this big mess while Mom and Claire allowed Dad to walk back into our life as easily as they let him walk out.

CHAPTER
Three

I SWIPED AT MY EYES AND TOLD MYSELF not to cry. I slid into the space between my bed and the window. It was just big enough for me to lean against the wall and hide. Sometimes Mom opened the door to look for me and didn't realize I was in this spot. I moved my hand around under my mattress until I found my walkie-talkie. I needed to talk to Lizzie, and it couldn't wait until school on Monday.

I pulled out the small black box and clicked it on. Mom refused to buy me a cell phone. She had a firm rule that I couldn't get one until I was in high school. I told her that's about as ridiculous as saying I didn't need food or water, to which Mom always replied that I was being too dramatic and should pick up the house phone if I needed to make a call. No, thank you. Claire's favorite hobby was eavesdropping, and it's kind of hard to trade secrets with your best friend when your sister might be listening to your every word.

That's why Lizzie and I came up with the greatest plan ever. We bought a set of walkie-talkies that could reach people up to six miles away.

If people heard we communicated this way they'd probably laugh and tell us no one really uses walkie-talkies, but they're pretty much the best solution ever because they solve the cell phone problem. I got the idea from a TV show about a group of guys who went hunting in the woods. They had superpowered industrial walkie-talkies to keep in contact. One of the guys wandered miles away chasing after a bear and fell and hurt his ankle. No one had a clue where he'd disappeared to, so his walkie-talkie saved him. He was able to tell the other guys where he was before the wild animals devoured him. It was all very dramatic and awesome. So maybe bears aren't going to eat us in our backyards, but you never know when an emergency late-night conversation might save one of our lives.

And I definitely needed one of those talks right now, because I was feeling miserable and, no matter what, Lizzie could make me feel better. It's as if she has some magical power to make me laugh, even when everything around me is a big, awful mess. She's possessed this talent since kindergarten, when we became friends after the two of us were paired up to practice writing the alphabet together.

I turned the power on and pressed the red button on the side of the walkie-talkie. "Hello, hello? Are you there?" Usually, if we wanted to talk, one of us would call the other's house phone and let it ring twice, but my family was still in the kitchen, so I hoped Lizzie would be waiting. "Lizzie? Talk to me!"

Luck was on my side, because the walkie-talkie crackled and Lizzie's voice came through.

"Where have you been?! Who goes MIA after finding out they got the lead in the school play?" she asked enthusiastically. Everything about Lizzie was enthusiastic. She always talked as if the most important thing in the world was happening right that very moment. I pictured her lying on her hot pink and white polka-dot comforter. I'm sure her blond hair was pulled back in a ponytail with her signature bow around it, and if her older sister, Amy, wasn't home, she'd be wearing a bunch of her eye shadow. Lizzie always practiced with her sister's makeup, something that constantly got her in trouble. The walkie-talkie crackled and her voice came through loud and clear. "I can't believe you didn't get on the walkie-talkie as soon as you got home."

"Sorry, things were kind of busy here," I told her, and tried not to sound as upset as I felt.

"You were too busy celebrating, weren't you?" She continued to blab on before I could correct her. "Let's talk about more interesting things, like what it's like to have the lead. Do you feel like a different person? Because you don't really sound like the same Grace to me."

I laughed despite everything. Lizzie was that good at making a person feel better. "I'm still me, but this is all pretty incredible."

"You're right it is. Beck and I were so excited when we saw your name. And you wouldn't believe how jealous Michelle was when she checked the cast list. I was standing by her, and she was fuming. It's about time someone knocked her off her throne." She said everything quickly, rushing through each sentence and not pausing to take a breath.

"What are you talking about?" My happy feeling suddenly evaporated, and I was left with a churning in my stomach like the time Mom poured me sour milk and I took a big gulp. Michelle and her friends were eighth graders who ruled the theater at Sloane Middle School. They were always getting the big parts in the plays and coming up with these amazing dance routines for the talent show each year. I definitely didn't want to get on Michelle's bad side—even though I was still pretty psyched that I'd beaten out the theater queen!

"Michelle totally wanted Snow White, and she wasn't happy when she found out she didn't get it. Anyway, how did your mom and Claire react? Did they go nuts when you told them about your part?"

"Not exactly," I said slowly, not sure how much I should tell Lizzie. "We kind of had a change of plans before I could tell them about the part."

"What are you talking about?"

I decided Lizzie should know; she knew everything about my family, the good, the bad, and the ugly. She'd seen Mom go ballistic on me for not emptying the dishwasher after asking me repeatedly to do it, and there was the time Claire got the flu and threw up all over the front hallway, and when Dad ran over the neighbors' garbage can and bolted instead of telling them. With how much time she spent in my house, there weren't a lot of secrets. Besides, Lizzie would kill me if I kept something like this to myself.

I took a deep breath and figured jumping right into it was

the best way to go about it. Kind of like pulling off a Band-Aid real fast; no sense dragging these things out forever.

"My dad is moving back in," I said. I told her what happened at dinner, every last bit of it.

"That's great news! Your dad moving in is a good thing."

"It most certainly isn't," I said a little too loudly. I lowered my voice, afraid my parents would hear me and come to check on me. "He showed up at dinner as if he never left us and things were A-OK."

"Talk about stealing your thunder," she said.

"My part doesn't seem like a big deal now," I said.

"It's a huge deal, Grace. You need to march right back downstairs and let them know how awesome you are."

I thought about how hard I had worked to get the lead. I went to drama camp for the past three summers, took voice lessons and ballet and tap lessons every week. Before I auditioned for the play, I watched the Disney version of *Snow White* over and over again, studying the movie as if I was preparing for a final exam. I'd worked so hard for this part, and now my parents' announcement had blown my hard work to pieces. It seemed so much smaller after the bomb my parents dropped on us.

"I don't know," I told Lizzie. I really didn't want to go back downstairs.

"I mean it," she said. "You need to be celebrating. I'm signing off and fully expect you to tell your family about your part."

"Okay, okay," I said, even though I had no intention of doing that. "I'll talk to you later."

"Congrats, Snow White!" Lizzie said one more time before I turned off the walkie-talkie. I stuck it back under the mattress and climbed onto my bed so I could stare out my window. It was growing dark. A man walked past with his dog, and Evan, my neighbor, hit a ball against his garage with a hockey stick. A car sped down the street, and two blackbirds sat on the side of the roof and pecked away at something. I stuck my tongue out at the birds.

"I bet you don't have to worry about other birds who try to move back into your nest," I told them. I draped my hand over my eyes and wondered what everyone was doing downstairs while I sat up here alone and tried to figure this all out myself.

CHAPTER
Four

DAD LEFT SHORTLY AFTER I FINISHED talking with Lizzie. He tried to say good-bye to me, but I hid under the patchwork quilt Grandma made me and pretended to sleep. I didn't know what to think about everything. I considered what it would be like to have Dad home. I remembered the good times: nights cracking peanuts while we watched the baseball game on TV; how Dad built campfires in our backyard so Lizzie, Beck, and I could roast marshmallows; and Dad and me taking Darby to the park. And it wasn't only the fun stuff that made him great, it was the other things too, like how he'd make me mashed potatoes from scratch when I had a sore throat and couldn't swallow anything else, or the night he slept in my room on the floor when Grandpa died and I was too scared to be alone. I remembered all the things that made Dad so great, and as much as I wanted to tell him I was glad he was coming back home, it scared me to think he might leave again.

I stayed under the covers until I heard Claire and Mom drive away the next morning. Claire had a soccer game, so the house was all mine for a few hours. I played on the computer, took a shower, and then made a big bowl of oatmeal. I covered it with about a pound of brown sugar, which was a big no-no when Mom was around but just what I needed. It was so much better than the plain oatmeal with fruit on top Mom would dish up for us. Blech! She'd try to convince us it was good, but Claire and I were smarter than that. It tasted like a bowlful of glue.

I took my food into the family room and sat smack-dab in the middle of the couch. Eating on the couch was another big no-no, but I'd make sure to hide the evidence before Mom got home. I settled down deep into the cushions with the TV remote in one hand, a spoon in the other, and the bowl of oatmeal balanced on my knee.

It was 11:57, and the midday news—the news station where Dad reported on the weather—would be on soon. I hadn't watched the news in a while, but today I needed to. The opening credits rolled and the two weekend anchors, Raymond and Emily, smiled at the camera. Emily's hair was teased up all high and she wore bright red lipstick.

"Good weekend afternoon, Cleveland," Raymond said. His teeth were so white, I wondered if they blinded the camera crew. "Thank you for joining us today. First up, a fire burned down a house in the middle . . ."

I zoned out and ate my oatmeal as the two of them droned on and on with the news. It wasn't until Emily introduced the weather that I paid attention.

"Next up, Chris Shaw is going to tell us if we should be pulling out the umbrellas this week." Emily smiled huge into the camera. I sat up in my seat and wished the commercials would finish faster.

I'd avoided watching Dad's news station during the past few months, but in the weeks right after he left, I studied him during the weather reports. He was on every afternoon except for Sundays. I'd tape the show while I was at school and watch it when I got home. I searched for clues in each newscast, trying to find something that helped make sense of my parents' separation. Mom didn't know I watched him; I always deleted the show from the DVR right after I watched.

After it became obvious that Dad wasn't returning, I stopped watching.

While Dad was describing the winds over the lake with big, sweeping hand gestures, the garage door opened and then slammed shut.

"We won, we won!" Claire screamed.

"Take off your shoes and go upstairs and change out of that dirty uniform. I don't want you messing up the floors," Mom yelled back. Not exactly the victory celebration Claire was probably hoping for, but that's our mom for you. I could hear Claire running up the steps.

I took the empty oatmeal bowl and quickly slid it under the couch so Mom wouldn't catch me eating where I wasn't supposed to. I'd get it later; it was better to hide the evidence now than face the wrath of Mom. I searched for the remote so I could change the channel before Mom caught me watching Dad, but I couldn't find it. I was checking under the cushions when Mom walked in.

"Looking for loose change?" she asked. "I'd be careful under there, you never know what you might find."

"Looking for lunch," I joked, and pulled out a shriveled-up carrot stick and held it high in the air as proof that she was right: there were questionable things lurking beneath the cushions.

Mom laughed with me. The two of us, just joking around, finally made me feel like this was the perfect moment to tell her about my part. "I have to tell you something," I said. "It's something really, really good."

"I like things that are really, really good," she said.

"Well . . . ," I started, but as I was about to tell her, the commercial ended and the news came back on.

"Good afternoon, Cleveland. Are you ready for a wet one this week?" Dad's voice boomed from the television and we both turned to look at him at the same time.

"The forecast shows it will be raining cats and dogs. After almost two weeks without rain, the grass is going to think tomorrow's storm is purrrrr-fect."

Mom made a little snort. "Your father makes the worst jokes in the world."

"People love him, though," I said, and it was as if the cameraman had read my mind, because suddenly Raymond's and Emily's faces appeared on the screen, the two laughing hard.

"Please don't tell my kids it'll be raining cats and dogs," Emily said. "They've been begging me to get a puppy."

"They might be getting their wish this week." Dad winked at the audience.

Mom and I both groaned, but you couldn't help but laugh. Dad was the highest-rated weatherman in Cleveland. The city loved Dad and he loved them back, which was why he always worked long hours doing his own broadcasts and covered special assignments, going to schools to give presentations and filling in for the other meteorologists when they took time off.

I fixed the cushions and plopped down. The TV changed to a commercial for McDonald's, and Mom sat too, putting her feet up on the coffee table, which was another big no-no in our house. I tilted my head and studied the rule-breaking stranger who looked like Mom.

"So about what you wanted to tell me . . . ," Mom said.

The moment felt less perfect now, but I couldn't *not* tell her. "Brace yourself," I said. "This news is going to rock your world."

"I like having my world rocked," my mom said, and leaned toward me. "Let me have it."

"I'm going to be Snow White in the school play!" I shouted.

Mom squealed and pulled me into a hug. "Oh, honey, I'm so, so happy for you."

"Me too! I can't even believe it," I said. I was so excited that I felt like I could burst.

"Why didn't you tell us last night that you got the part

of Snow White?" she asked, and I could see the hurt in her eyes. She was still smiling, but I knew her better. It was the same look she used to give Claire and me after she hung up the phone from a conversation with Dad. The calls where she tried not to raise her voice or say anything beyond the usual instructions of when we'd go to visit with him. "We could have spent the evening celebrating."

I shrugged and played with the cuff of my shirt. Every time I thought about my role, I thought about crying, too. How was it possible to be happy and sad at the same time? "I didn't feel much like celebrating last night."

Mom's smile disappeared and the tone of her voice got more serious. "Last night was a bit of a surprise, wasn't it?"

Really? Of course last night was a surprise. Dad hadn't been in our house for almost a year and suddenly he was the guest of honor at dinner.

"I'm sorry we sprang it on you and Claire, but we wanted to tell you together."

I played with the fringe on one of the cushions and stared at the TV. The car commercial made me wish I was old enough to drive so I could get far, far away from here.

"Having your dad here is going to be a good thing. Don't you think?"

I shrugged again. Did it have to be a good thing or a bad thing?

"Think about all the junk food your dad will bring back in the house," Mom joked, poking me in the side like she does when she wants me to laugh. The thing is, this wasn't a laughing matter, but Mom didn't seem to realize that. She acted as if this talk would make everything better. "It will be good to have him home."

"Claire seems to think it will," I said.

"And so should you. We need to be a family again," Mom said, and I nodded to make her happy. "So do you feel okay about Dad moving back in?"

"Sure," I said, because that's what Mom wanted to hear, but my mind was screaming, *No, no, no.*

"I'm glad we talked about this," she said. She brushed a piece of hair away from my face and then squeezed my shoulder.

"Me too," I said, but it didn't feel like we talked about much. Mom might have thought I understood things, but inside I was still scared and confused. Why did Dad decide to come back now? If you loved someone, why would you walk away from them in the first place? And if you walked away once, what would keep you from walking away again?

CHAPTER
Five

I WAS EXCITED ABOUT MY PART IN *SNOW White*, but Dad's news made it hard to focus on my new role. He moved in on Sunday and it felt strange having him back in the house. It seemed as if the only important thing now was Dad returning home, so it was a relief to go back to school on Monday.

The cast list was still posted, and I'm not ashamed to admit I walked past it on my way to every single class, which is where Michelle and her gang found me after fourth period. I was staring at my name with a goofy grin on my face when they walked up behind me. Michelle, Katie, and Susan. The girls who ran the theater. The leads and solos always went to them. They were amazing and they knew it.

I remembered what Lizzie had told me when we talked the other night about Michelle being upset that I got the part of Snow White. I faked a smile that I hope looked real, because I sure as heck didn't feel happy right now. More like scared, but I wasn't about to let these girls see that.

"Congratulations on your part," Michelle said in a way that didn't feel very congratulatory. She stood with her hands on her hips as if waiting for me to say something. Katie and Susan snickered on either side of her.

"Um, thanks," I said, because what else was I supposed to do? I hoisted my pink backpack onto my shoulder and glanced down the hallway, where people were heading toward their classes, hoping the girls would take the hint that we needed to get moving or we'd be late for fifth period. They didn't.

"We all know why you got the part," Katie said while Michelle nodded.

We? I wondered if there was some kind of announcement I'd missed.

"You do?" I asked, and hoped they couldn't tell how bad my knees were shaking. I breathed in and out deeply, a trick I learned to do to calm my butterflies before going onstage.

"Isn't it obvious?" Michelle laughed, but it sounded more like a witch cackling. "It's because of your dark black hair and pale ghost skin. Mrs. Hiser only cast you because you look like Snow White."

My hand automatically went up to my hair, and I wound a piece of it around my finger. I loved my black hair. Mom and Claire had it too, and people were always telling us how lucky we were to have such beautiful hair. But suddenly it felt like the worst color in the world.

"I don't think that's how she——" I started, but Michelle cut me off.

"She'll realize soon enough what a mistake she made casting a seventh grader as the lead." She wrinkled her nose when she said "seventh grader," as if it were something gross and disgusting that she stomped under her foot.

It wasn't until the three of them walked away that I remembered seeing Michelle's name next to the role of the Evil Queen. Funny, if she thought Mrs. Hiser gave me my part based on my appearance, it also seemed like Mrs. Hiser was dead-on in casting Michelle based on her personality.

CHAPTER
Six

LIZZIE AND BECK MET ME OUTSIDE THE theater at the end of the school day, before our first rehearsal. It was a good thing, because after what Michelle said, I didn't know if I'd have the guts to walk in by myself. I told myself repeatedly that I had earned the part of Snow White. I was good, and there wasn't any other reason why Mrs. Hiser had picked me for the role. I tried to convince myself of that fact, but I wasn't doing a good job.

"So are you ready for your read-through as the star of the show?" Beck asked with a smile. His hair was wild and curly, and he wore his trademark outfit of green Converse sneakers, a plaid shirt, and big black glasses (which were fake and for show, but I've been sworn to secrecy about that). Beck was one of my favorite people in the world because he didn't let other people bother him. He did what he wanted to, even if it was different. Things like drinking black coffee and carrying a big brown leather murse (translation: "man purse," but he would kill me if he heard me call it that) instead of a book bag. Or listening to music that was popular when our parents were our age.

"Seriously, I'm surprised you're still talking to us," Lizzie joked. "Most actors forget the little people when they get a lead."

"Whatever," Beck said, squeezing between the two of us and slinging a hand over each of our shoulders. He smelled like the aftershave my uncle Dan wore, which made me laugh to myself. Beck did not need to shave anything yet, except maybe the wild mop of hair on his head. "I hardly think Ensemble Member and Grumpy the Dwarf are little parts."

"You're right," I told him. "Can you imagine how awful it would be if *Snow White* had one less person in the ensemble and all the dwarfs were happy? It would be a disaster. You two totally make the show."

"We do, don't we?" Lizzie asked. "I'm going to rock my ensemble role."

She broke away from the two of us, puffed out her chest, and walked down the hallway as if she were on a runway. Her blond ponytail and purple ribbon swished from side to side. Beck snapped his fingers and hummed the lyrics to one of my favorite dance songs. A few kids stopped to watch as Lizzie turned around and headed back toward us, swinging her hips. Lizzie was a star whether she wanted to be or not, even though she always asked for the smaller roles in the plays. She said she loved being a part of everything, but what she didn't love was memorizing lines. She's probably the only person in the world who didn't want to get a lead.

"I'm ready," I said. I pushed the conversation with Michelle and her cronies to the back of my mind. "Let's do this."

The three of us headed into the theater. The excitement of our first rehearsal made me giddy. The read-through was one of my favorite parts of being in a play. The scripts would be handed out, highlighters would be passed around, and we'd read straight through from beginning to end. It's kind of like Christmas, because you never know how many lines you'll get, so when I come across one of my own, it's like opening a gift. There is nothing better than dragging the highlighter over a sentence. In the past, Beck and I had talked about the day we would became one of those people who have so many lines, they complain to their friends that they can't keep up with the highlighting. Secretly, I was bursting with excitement at the fact that this would be me today. I'd walk out of rehearsal with my script covered in fluorescent lines!

We climbed the steps to the stage and headed to our usual spot in the far left corner, away from where the director always sat. If you didn't have a lead, rehearsals were more about sitting around than anything else. That's why this area was the perfect place. We could talk quietly and not bother anyone if we kept our voices down. Except, today I did have a lead.

"Maybe you should sit over there." Beck gestured toward an old, worn-out couch occupied by Michelle, Katie, and Susan. They held highlighters and sat straight up, beaming at Mrs. Hiser. There was no way I was joining that group. I may have enough guts to get up onstage in front of hundreds of people, but when it came to facing the three of them, all my courage disappeared.

"Um, I think I'll pass," I said, and sat down with the two of them. "I'll stick with the two of you. Nothing has changed; I just have a different part this time."

"A different part?" Beck said, and stretched out his legs. Purple-and-black-striped socks peeked out from under his pants. "Try a bigger part."

38

"Okay, everyone, let's begin," Mrs. Hiser said as she clapped her hands to get our attention. There were a lot of us. Sloane Middle School's policy was that everyone could be a part of the fall play, which meant about forty people were on the stage. Mrs. Hiser always directed the show. She'd been in charge since she started working at our school more than twenty years ago, fresh out of a performing arts school in New York City. I loved her. She had bright red hair that went halfway down her back and she was super tiny, but her voice could reach from the stage to the back of the theater when she wanted to be heard. She was the choir teacher during the day, but from everything she knows about acting, you can tell that she grew up on the stage. "We have a lot to get through today and not a lot of time. For those of you who don't know one another, you'll get there eventually. However, I do want to introduce some of the people you'll be seeing a lot of."

Lizzie nudged me. "That's you, girl. Everyone is going to know your name."

"Let's meet our Prince Charming, James Lowe, first, since he's right next to me," Mrs. Hiser said. She turned to James, and I swear, every girl in the room swooned. And who wouldn't? James was super-duper cute. He had thick brown hair that always fell in his eyes. He did this head-shake thing where he'd toss it back. And he's not only a rock star in the theater, he's kind of a rock star in real life, too. He started a band with four other guys and they call themselves Detroit Avenue, after the street the three of them live on. James is the guitarist, and maybe the band isn't selling out arenas, but they were amazing at our school talent show. We all joke about the "triple threat" in the theater, which is someone who can sing, dance, and act, but what do you call someone who can do all that *and* rock out with a band?

And now this boy was the leading man to my leading lady. That fact alone would probably make me the envy of the school, and I'm not going to deny that I didn't mind. Nope, not one little bit, thank you very much. I blushed and sat up a little straighter.

"Lucky you," a girl in my grade named Annie said, leaning over Beck to talk to me. She was playing a townsperson, along with Lizzie. She winked at me. "I'd give anything to act out the final scene of this play with James."

"The final scene?" I asked, trying to remember what happened at the very end of the play, but before I could figure it out, Lizzie elbowed me again and pointed toward Mrs. Hiser.

"Grace, wave your hand so the group can meet you," Mrs. Hiser said, and it seemed as if she was trying hard not to laugh, especially since everyone was already looking at me.

I stuck my hand in the air, and the stack of colorful fabric and bead bracelets I thought were so cool this morning slid down to my elbow.

"I think our *little* Snow White is going to need to learn how to pay attention, or Grace will miss all her cues during the show," Michelle said to the group. She made sure to enunciate the word "little" good and loud, even though she was only a year older than me.

"I think our Evil Queen needs to learn how to be a *little* nicer to the lead so Grace doesn't accidently forget a line and cut out some of your big speeches," Beck shot back, and a few of the younger cast members stared at him with wide eyes. I couldn't believe he said that, but I wanted to high-five him for sticking up for me. At least until I snuck a look at Michelle and saw that her eyes were tiny slits, her lips pulled into a tight, thin line.

"Okay, that's enough. We're not going to have behavior like this in our show or you won't be *in* our show," Mrs. Hiser said. She focused on both Beck and Michelle long enough to make each squirm. When she seemed satisfied that they had gotten the message, she continued to introduce the leads while the stage manager passed out our scripts. When she handed me my copy, I swear I felt a bolt of electricity go through me, as if the paper held magical powers. I couldn't wait to see my lines, the words that would take me from the real world and transport me to a land far, far away.

We read all the way through. We didn't act anything out or move around; today was about hearing the story and getting to know our characters. The process took two hours, and I loved every minute of it. I was a highlighting fool, and I swear smoke was going to billow out of my marker. That's how fast I was moving to keep up. At one point Beck elbowed me and asked if I needed him to get me some ice, because he was sure my wrist must be sore from all the work it was doing. I grinned and tried not to show how truly awesome this all was.

At least, it *was* awesome.

Until I saw the words that changed my life forever.

They were on the second-to-last page, written as stage directions. They were at the very bottom, in slanted italics.

Prince Charming wakes Snow White with a kiss.

My world came crashing down with two words.

A kiss?!

What Annie had said now made sense. I was going to

have to kiss James. I glanced quickly at him. He looked at me, too, but before anything else could happen, I turned away. I felt my face heating up, and I was sure I was blushing bright red. Because the thing is, Snow White might be perfectly fine with kissing Prince Charming, but I was a whole different story.

I had never kissed a boy in my entire life. Not even close. And now, written right here on the paper in front of me, it seemed as if I was going to get my first kiss in front of an audience full of people with none other than Sloane Middle School's megahottie, James Lowe.

CHAPTER
Seven

LIZZIE'S MOM DROPPED ME OFF AFTER rehearsal, and I took my time heading into the house. Next door, Evan was outside with his dog, and I considered running into his house and hiding out for a while. It was sure to be more normal than what was going on inside of mine.

I reached my front steps, took a deep breath, and walked through the door. There was a big bouquet of yellow daisies and red roses on the table and a card with my name on it. Mom's big, loopy handwriting congratulated me on my part, and everyone had signed it. She made sure to put lots of hearts and smiley faces.

I bent down to smell the flowers as Dad walked in.

Operation Pucker Up

He stood in the doorway in his business suit, his collar unbuttoned and maroon tie loosened. The gold watch on his wrist flashed in the sunlight that streamed through the window, and I remembered how when I was younger I used to put it on and slide it up and down my arm.

"There's my Snow White. I'm so proud of you, honey," he said, and for a brief moment it was the way it used to be. He smiled so his eyes crinkled around the corners, and I wanted to jump up and down and tell him how excited I was about the part. But the feeling disappeared the instant Mom and Claire joined him. Dad put his arm around Mom's waist and Claire clung to his leg like a little kid, even though she was eight years old. How was it so easy for them to do that? To accept him back home and not worry about what would happen if he got tired of us again?

"How was your first rehearsal?" Mom asked. "We want to hear all about it. You're going to make an amazing Snow White."

"Will you move to Disney World to live in the castle?" Claire asked.

I bent down so I was on her level and pulled her away from Dad into a hug of my own. "No way, Claire Bear. I'm staying here with you. You're nuts if you think I'd ditch you and Mom." I looked at Dad and knew he understood what I'd left out.

"We can't wait to see you up onstage," Mom said.

Dad pointed at the bouquet. "Who says flowers should only be given to the actress at the end of the show, right? I wanted to be the first one to give you flowers to congratulate you for the performance I know is going to be fabulous."

Suddenly the smell from the flowers seemed overpowering and made me sick. My stomach twisted and turned as if it was doing cartwheels. I did not want flowers from Dad, because all I could think about was the play he missed. The flowers he didn't give me the first time around.

Claire walked over and touched the petals on one of the daisies.

"You can have these," I said to her. "They're so pretty, and I know you'll take good care of them."

"Really?" she asked, and I nodded. I glanced at Dad and I could see the hurt in his eyes. I wished I had the courage to tell him why I didn't want these flowers, but my own hurt still stung too deep. Instead, I grabbed the vase.

"Should we put them in your room?" I asked my sister.

"Yes!" she shouted, and hopped from one foot to the other.

"Grace, Dad got them for *you*," Mom said, but I pretended

not to hear her. I was becoming a great pretender these days, both on and off the stage.

"Mom," Claire said. "They are *my* flowers now. Grace said so. I'll take good care of them; I promise."

"I know you will," I said, and pulled gently on her braid. "Let's get these up to your room. I think we should put them right on top of your dresser so you see them first thing in the morning. Sound good?"

Claire nodded and giggled, super excited at the thought of her own bouquet of flowers. I picked up the vase and let my sister push her way past Mom and Dad, and I followed, free from them. I felt as if I could breathe again.

CHAPTER
Eight

THE NEXT MORNING, I WAS WAITING outside for the bus when Evan walked out of his house. He threw some stuff into the back of his family's SUV and tried to open the passenger-side door. When he figured out it was locked, he leaned against the side of it instead, facing my house.

I was surprised to see him still at home. He was always gone by the time I headed outside to catch my bus. Mom joked about how early his family got moving, while we always seemed to be running around, rushed and disorganized.

He was in eighth grade at Lakewood Academy, the private school in our town, and had moved here a few months ago. Lizzie thought he was totally crushworthy, and Mom was always telling me that he seemed like a nice boy and how I should go over to get to know him, but what was I supposed to do? Knock on the door and ask if Evan wanted to come over and hang out? Yeah, that's not awkward. Besides, I didn't know him at all—what would I even say to him? And it wasn't like he was coming over to my house to meet me. I may be able to get up onstage and belt out a solo, but when it came to boys, I flubbed my words like someone who found out she had to kiss Prince Charming.

But today I didn't need to worry about that, because Evan was the one who came over to where I stood on the driveway, as if we chatted every morning and this wasn't unusual at all. He rubbed his hands together quickly and blew on them. "It's getting cold out here, huh?"

I nodded. "Some of the leaves are already turning colors in our backyard."

"Same with our house," he said, and paused, a conversation started and then stalled. We stood facing each other, neither of us knowing what to say, probably because we never said anything to each other.

I glanced down at my scruffy tennis shoes and then at Evan's brown dress shoes. He wore his school uniform, navy blue pants and a white dress shirt. A tie hung around his neck, but it wasn't knotted. His short brown hair was still wet from his shower, and he stood close enough to me that I could smell his fresh and soapy scent. I felt like a slob in my jeans and sweatshirt. Why couldn't I have run into him when I was wearing one of my power outfits for school? The clothes I save for those days when I want to wow the world. The clothes that make me feel as if I can conquer anything. I glanced back at my shoes and the frayed shoelaces that hung off the side. Today's outfit was definitely lacking.

"So what's up?" he finally asked.

"The sky," I said automatically, and cringed. Ugh! What was I thinking? It was a phrase Mom, Claire, and I always used. A phrase that should have stayed between the three of us.

Evan laughed in a way that made me think he was only being polite, which was even worse than telling me straight-out what a dork I was.

"My mom's taking forever to get moving today," he said. "Usually I'm the one she has to wait for in the morning."

"At least you have a ride. I beg my mom all the time to drive me so I don't have to ride the big yellow clunker, but she refuses."

"Your dad won't drive you?"

I paused. "I doubt it," I said.

"Mom said he moved back in," he blurted. He looked away, embarrassed.

I bit my bottom lip and stared at the ground. Great. Other people had noticed that Dad was back. It was probably the talk of the neighborhood.

"Yeah," I said, even though it wasn't any of his business. Mom would call him a busybody right now and tell him to take a long walk off a short pier.

"My grandma moved into our house a few weeks ago," he said, and kicked a rock on the driveway.

"She did?"

"She's too sick to live on her own."

"It's probably nice to have her around," I said, because I didn't know what else to say.

"Yes and no. There's a whole list of rules now. We have to be quiet because of her, eat earlier, and not watch TV late. It isn't the same anymore." Evan shoved his hands into his pants pocket, and his green eyes focused on my own.

His front door banged shut, and we both turned toward Evan's mom, who rushed down the driveway with her hands full of folders and her purse slipping off her shoulder. Her cell phone was up to her ear and she jabbered away as her heels made clacking noises across the sidewalk.

 51

"That's my ride," Evan said. I felt a weird twinge of disappointment. I wanted to keep talking to him. I wanted to tell him how I understood what he meant about his house suddenly not being his house anymore. And just talk about other stuff too. But instead I pointed down the street.

"My ride should be rumbling up soon."

"The yellow clunker." He laughed, climbed into the SUV, and gave me a little wave.

I waved back and turned to his house, wondering if we actually had more in common than I thought.

CHAPTER
Nine

THERE WAS NO ESCAPING THE KISS. LIZZIE was talking about it as soon as I got to math that afternoon. I raced to class, because I wanted to tell her about how Dad was trying to get Claire and me to go hiking in Cleveland Metroparks this weekend, something I certainly did not want to do. I needed someone to agree and help me find a way out of it, because Mom thought it was a great idea and promised to pack a special lunch for us to bring. Lizzie would understand, or so I thought. It quickly became obvious that the only thing she cared about now was James and me.

"Have you thought about what kind of lip gloss you're going to wear when he kisses you?" she asked.

"Actually, I wanted to tell you about what my dad—"

"Because fruit punch is probably the best flavor. Think about it . . . guys love fruit punch. Remember when they drank both the containers full of it last year at Field Day? I think that's your best choice."

I felt a tiny twinge of hurt that Lizzie wasn't listening to me. I could usually depend on her to be there when I needed her, but right now it seemed Lizzie was way more excited about her favorite subject in the world: kissing.

She claimed to be an expert in all things kissing. Not because she'd kissed a lot of boys (the two of us together bring the grand total to zero), but because she could teach a class on how to do everything that was involved in the perfect kiss. She knew which way to turn your head, when to close your eyes, and what to do with your hands. She could tell you what a kiss good-bye looked like, how to say hello after being apart, and exactly how long to kiss if you weren't quite sure you wanted to kiss the person again. She was even an expert on what type of lipstick to wear so you didn't get it all over the boy you were kissing.

I have no reason not to accept Lizzie's knowledge as truth. She might not have put all these tips into practice, but she'd studied them for years. She knows it all.

How?

Reality TV shows.

The best teachers in the world, according to Lizzie.

Her mom is addicted to them, especially the ones where a whole bunch of girls are competing against one another for one single guy. Every time I'm at Lizzie's house, her mom seems to be watching one of these shows.

"I saw an episode where one of the girls got a rose from the guy by trailing her hand down the side of his face," Lizzie whispered after Mrs. Gutman passed out a worksheet where we were supposed to be dividing mixed fractions, but instead of focusing on the work, I couldn't stop worrying about this kiss with James. I had no idea how much time I had until Mrs. Hiser made us practice the scene. I guess it didn't matter, because no amount of time was going to make me ready. James would know as soon as I kissed him that I'd never done it before. He'd probably tell the whole world what a lousy kisser I was and no one would ever kiss me again. Lizzie, on the other hand, wasn't sympathetic to my problem. She was trying to school me in the fine art of laying a big one on someone. "He couldn't resist her when she leaned in for a kiss."

"I'm not about to trail my hand down James's face," I told her. "He'd think I was nuts."

"I'm telling you, it worked. I totally thought the guy was going to pick another girl, but when she put that move on him, he was all about giving her a rose. It was magic."

"Maybe my mom should have watched that show—it might have kept my parents from separating," I said, and waited for her to say something in return. But instead she went back to talking about James as if I hadn't even brought up my parents. This was the second time today I had tried to talk to her about my parents, but it seemed as if she was more interested in the play and what was going to happen onstage than in my real life.

"I wonder how this kiss is going to go down in rehearsal. Do you think Mrs. Hiser will make you do it like it's part of the script? Can you picture that? You're reading and reading and then boom, time to lean in for the kiss as if it's nothing!"

"Why are you making me think about this stuff?" I asked way too loud. Some of my classmates turned and stared.

"Grace and Lizzie, is there something you care to share with the class?" Mrs. Gutman asked, and stood over us, silencing all conversation.

"No," I said, and shook my head back and forth so fast, I thought it would fly off my shoulders. I certainly *did not* want to share our conversation.

"Then I suggest you get back to focusing on math," she said, and moved away.

I slid down into my seat and rubbed my temples with my hands. This was all too much. There was no way I could conquer this kiss with James, especially when I put together everything involved in a kiss. It wasn't only my lips. No way, that would make it too easy. I needed to worry about it all: the lips, breath, noses, hands, chins, and probably a bunch of other things that I didn't know about but would have to figure out.

"I've got it!" Lizzie whispered, and I thought she was going to jump out of her seat from excitement. Instead, she leaned toward me, beckoning me with her finger to do the same. I hesitated. I wanted to forget this conversation altogether, especially since Mrs. Gutman had already yelled at us once, but Lizzie wouldn't leave me alone. I gave in and leaned the rest of the way so she could whisper in my ear. "What if James wasn't your first kiss?"

"What do you mean?"

"What if we got someone else to kiss you?"

"Someone else?" I couldn't even handle James kissing me, now I needed to add another person to my list?

"It's brilliant. We'll call it Operation Pucker Up!"

"Operation what?" My head was spinning as I tried to figure out what she meant.

"Operation Pucker Up. We'll find someone for you to kiss so you can get your first kiss out of the way and gain some practice. When James finally lays one on you, you'll be an old pro! He won't be able to resist you. He'll wish that wicked witch had given you a whole basketful of poisonous apples so he could keep kissing you over and over again."

"I don't think I'll get that good," I said. I couldn't even handle kissing Prince Charming, and now Lizzie thought I could kiss another boy too? Um, no. Plus, who would I even kiss?

"It makes perfect sense. I'm a genius." Lizzie sat back and crossed her hands over her chest. She looked happy with herself.

"I'm not sure about that. Where are we going to find someone to kiss me? Remember? The problem we have to begin with is that I've never had anyone to kiss."

She answered with a smirk on her face. "That one is easy."

And I knew. I just knew the name she was going to say, like twins can communicate without talking. Lizzie and I were like that. We've been friends so long that we know each other's thoughts before we say them. But this was one thought I wish I didn't know.

"No way," I told her.

"What?" she asked, acting all innocent, as if she had no idea what I was talking about.

"I'm not kissing Beck. No way, nohow. Beck is our *friend*. He's not someone we kiss."

"Come on, Grace. It's perfect. He'll totally help us, and unless he's been lying to us, he's never kissed anyone either. You two could practice with each other. It would be sort of sweet."

I gave her a look that made it clear that it would be anything but sweet.

"Not going to happen," I said. "It would be completely weird between us afterward."

"You'll be fine. It's two friends helping each other out in an emergency. Beck would do anything for us, including kissing you if he had to."

"Oh, like I'm so horrible to kiss that someone *has* to do it," I said, even though I knew that wasn't what Lizzie meant by her comment. And she was right, Beck would help me out. The three of us did that type of thing for one another. If one of us needed something, the other two stepped up. Like the time Beck got a big zit in between his eyes right before class pictures. We showed him how to cover it with concealer and never told a soul he was wearing makeup. Or when Lizzie was sick with strep throat and we brought over pints of ice cream and our favorite Disney movies. We tied bandannas around our mouths and noses so we could keep her company and not worry about getting sick. And when Dad walked out on Mom, the two of them never, ever mentioned it to anyone so the rest of the grade would think everything in my life was perfectly normal, even when it was far from it.

"It wouldn't feel right. He's Beck. And we don't kiss Beck."

"It wouldn't be real kissing. It would be practice kissing. Like when we have rehearsals."

"We made a pact that we'd never have crushes on him, don't you remember?"

"Don't you want to impress James with your kissing skills? You wouldn't go onstage in front of an audience without practicing first."

"I don't know," I told her, but what she said was beginning to make sense. We put in weeks and weeks of rehearsals before a show; I could think of kissing Beck in the same way. It wouldn't mean anything but practice. "He probably wouldn't agree to it."

"Leave the convincing to me. I'll talk to him. You just need to put on lots of lip gloss to get your lips ready for Operation Pucker Up. You'll be a kissing master in no time."

Mrs. Gutman stopped in front of us and gave us the look only teachers can give that means we need to get to work or else. I was relieved when Lizzie picked up her pencils and focused on trying to figure out a problem. I did the same, but thought about how I was doomed when figuring out division was the better option than the conversation I was having with Lizzie.

CHAPTER
Ten

DINNER THAT NIGHT WAS SPAGHETTI, garlic bread, and awkward conversation. Dad told a story about how during the newscast that day, a man on the editing team stood in the background behind the anchors so he could be seen by the viewers and had a whole conversation on his cell phone while they were live on the air.

"He was fighting with whoever was on the phone. Waving his hands and shaking his head. He had no idea that the camera could pick him up," Dad said, and Mom and Claire joined in with his laughing.

Ever since he moved back in, Dad has made it a point to eat dinner with us, because part of the reason my parents fought before he left was because Mom got upset about all the time Dad would spend at his job. We used to always eat together, but then he began to miss dinners. At first it was only once or twice a week, and it didn't seem like that big a deal, but in those final months, when Mom and Dad fought all the time, we were lucky if he ate with us at all.

The phone rang two times and stopped—Lizzie's and my signal that we needed to turn on our walkie-talkies.

"Can I be excused?" I asked Mom.

"You hardly ate anything," Dad pointed out.

"I snacked earlier. I was starving when I got home from rehearsal, so Mom made me a peanut butter and jelly sandwich. We used to eat at five, not at six thirty," I told him. He worked later than Mom did because he helped prepare some of the work for the evening weatherman. Now that Dad was back, Mom magically shifted dinnertime so we could all sit and eat together, pretending to be the big happy family we most definitely were not. "Can I please go upstairs? I have homework to do."

Mom sighed, but she was willing to give up the fight. "Yes, go ahead, but I was hoping you'd tell us about rehearsal today. You've hardly talked about the play."

I was up and out of my seat as soon as she said yes, especially since rehearsal was the last thing I wanted to think about.

Today we worked on blocking, which meant Mrs. Hiser walked us through where to move and stand during each scene. We worked on a part in the play with the dwarfs, which meant Beck had been there. He was the same Beck in a blue flannel shirt and Converse, but I didn't feel like the same Grace.

I kept glancing at him when he wasn't paying attention and thinking about what it would be like to kiss him. Probably super awkward and totally unromantic.

Lizzie told me she planned to talk to him after rehearsal, and that made it impossible to focus. Even though the three of us were always there for one another, I wondered if Beck would actually agree to kiss me. Our friendship with Beck started in the second grade when we met in the community theater's production of *The Wizard of Oz*. The three of us were cast as Munchkins (a.k.a. the role every short kid who didn't freeze onstage during auditions got). We were paired with a girl named Laurel who kept trying to step in front of the three of us so the audience would be able to see her best. We were supposed to stay in the little group our director had positioned us in, but she'd walk ahead of us and throw her arms out, keeping us behind her. It got so bad that I wanted a tornado to blow past and land a house on her so she'd stop. Beck had finally had enough after she blocked the audience's view of us on opening night. When she was in front of him, he "accidentally" lost his footing, and his prop, a big candy lollipop, got stuck in her hair. The scene was moving too fast, and she didn't have time to pull it out. She was forced to follow the yellow brick road with a huge sucker tangled in her curls. It took everything within the three of us not to laugh. One of the stagehands needed to cut the lollipop out after the scene, and she ended up missing a chunk of hair and most of the second act. Laurel never stepped in front of us again, and Beck, Lizzie, and I became instant friends. The kind of friends who would do anything for one another. But I wasn't sure if kissing was included in that.

I locked my bedroom door, pulled out the walkie-talkie, and slipped into my secret hiding spot against the wall. Lizzie was waiting for me as soon as I turned on the power.

"Grace?" Her voice buzzed through the speaker.

"I'm here."

"Operation Pucker Up is a go. It's been put into action!"

"How?" I asked, and felt my stomach start to twist and turn.

"Beck agreed to kiss you. Tomorrow, before school. He said he'll meet you in the theater, backstage by the prop shelves before homeroom at seven thirty. Be there and be prepared to have your life changed."

I pressed the side button to tell her no way, nohow, this was not a good idea, but all I got was the nasty beep telling me she had turned off her walkie-talkie. The little sneak left so I couldn't argue. I picked up a pillow and threw it against the wall. That was so typical of Lizzie! Of course she'd disappear before I could say no.

I fell asleep that night and had nightmares of giant, shiny red lips with little feet on the bottom chasing me, and of people pointing and laughing instead of trying to help me. If that wasn't a sign of things to come, I don't know what was.

CHAPTER
Eleven

HOW EXACTLY DOES ONE DRESS FOR A first kiss? I asked myself the next morning. I had a feeling the fashion magazines didn't give advice on an outfit like that, but it's what I needed right now. The school bus would arrive at my house in ten minutes, and it looked like my closet had exploded. I stood in the middle of my room while every outfit I owned surrounded me on the floor. And not one of them was right.

I needed to be careful not to give Beck the wrong message with my outfit. He needed to know this was a friend helping a friend. But I also didn't want him to think I didn't care. This was my first kiss, after all, and I was sure that when I

was old and told my grandchildren about this day, I'd want
to tell them I'd worn something cute. That meant my T-shirt
with the giant Cookie Monster face was definitely out of the
running. "I have nothing!" I yelled, so loud that Dad stuck his
head into my room. Great. Just what I needed.

"Everything okay?" he asked. He was dressed for work
in gray pants and a white collared shirt. There was a piece of
shaving cream still on his cheek.

"No," I said. I wanted him out of my room. He was the
last person I needed to witness my breakdown over my lack
of clothes to wear.

"Can I help?"

"No," I said again. How many times did I have to keep
repeating that until he got the hint that I didn't want him here?

"It looks to me like you're trying to find an outfit."

I switched tactics. Maybe if I didn't talk, he'd leave.

Nope. Not a chance.

Instead, he walked over to one of my piles and dug
around in it. He pulled out a long-sleeve navy blue top and
faded jeans. He went through my closet and grabbed the pair
of green flats Mom bought me when we were at the mall a few
weeks ago. They were the color of grass on a brilliant summer day, and I'd loved how different they were when I tried

them on at the store. I hadn't worn them yet, though, because once I got home with them, I didn't feel brave enough to wear shoes that bright. But somehow, when Dad put them with the simple top and jeans, they went perfectly.

"What do you think?" he asked. "Not bad for a man who only wears suits, huh?"

I shrugged, but gave a little nod. "It might work."

"I'll set them right here," Dad said, draping the top and pants over the back of my desk chair and leaving the shoes on the floor. "If you need anything else, shout."

"Thanks," I said quietly.

He backed out of the room, and I was left wondering what just happened. I checked the clock. The bus would be here in five minutes. I put the clothes on and told myself I was only wearing them because I didn't have time to find anything else, but when I stood in front of the mirror I smiled at myself. The outfit was super cute. I didn't want to admit it, but the truth was, I looked like a girl who was ready to get her first kiss.

CHAPTER
Twelve

BECK WAS A TOTAL OF ELEVEN MINUTES AND twenty-three seconds late (not that I was counting or anything).

After waiting four minutes, I got nervous and my armpits got all gross and sweaty, so I dug two Kleenex out of my bag and stuck them under my shirt to appear cool, calm, and collected when Beck arrived.

When he was seven minutes late, I started pacing back and forth in the little room backstage. There wasn't much room to move. It took five steps to cross the room, but I needed to do something because I couldn't stop my mind from moving a million miles an hour. I had pretty much convinced myself that he wasn't going to show up.

After nine minutes of being alone in the dark, I decided this was a horrible idea. I should have never agreed to Operation Pucker Up in the first place.

Just as I was about to quit and tell Lizzie that OPU was not happening, Beck appeared.

I watched him as he ducked behind the heavy maroon curtains to get backstage. His sweatshirt was unzipped over one of those T-shirts that look like a tuxedo top. I wondered if that was his way of dressing up for the occasion, and I laughed to myself.

When he saw me, he smiled so the dimple in his right cheek came out and he looked like regular Beck.

"I'm here to change your life with my lips," he joked. "Are you sure you're up for this? Because after I lay one on you, I have a feeling that you won't ever be the same again."

Beck attempted to make muscles in his arms, and I relaxed.

He put his bag on one of the prop shelves and unzipped it. "I've come with supplies."

"Why do we need supplies?"

He pulled a bunch of items out and laid them on the shelf. "You can never be too prepared. I've got a toothbrush and toothpaste. Did you brush today?"

"Of course I brushed today. They're squeaky clean," I told him, and showed him my chompers. What I didn't say was that I brushed them two times, flossed, and used mouthwash. A girl can never be too careful, right?

"Good. I also have breath mints, ChapStick, and a chocolate bar."

"A chocolate bar?"

"We need to celebrate our first kiss." Beck stopped talking and stared at me funny.

"What?" I asked.

He tilted his head to the side, squinted, and appeared confused. "Are you wearing makeup?"

"No!" I interjected quickly, before he could investigate further. "That's silly. Why would I be wearing makeup?" Okay, so maybe I swiped some of Mom's mascara and eyeliner. I tried to put it on the best I could, but it felt funny and foreign. My eyes were heavy, and I kept wanting to rub them, forgetting that it was the mascara making them feel sticky.

"You don't look like yourself."

"Maybe that's better, right? This is kind of weird."

Beck shrugged. "Weird, but not in a bad way."

I narrowed my eyes. What? Was he talking as if maybe he wanted to do this in a way that was more than friends? This was supposed to be a favor. One friend helping another friend out.

I pushed those thoughts from my mind. I had a job to do, and I was going to "man up," as Lizzie would say, and get it done. I pointed at my watch. "We better, uh, we need to get moving. The bell is going to ring."

Beck nodded and cleared his throat. "How should we do this?"

"Let's count to three," I said, even though I had no idea what we were supposed to do.

"Okay, counting makes sense. One," Beck said, and took a step closer to me. He was fidgety and tapped his fingers against his leg. I wondered if he was as nervous as I was.

"Two," I said, and took a deep breath.

"Three," he said, and we leaned in close and our heads slammed into each other with a clunk so loud it could probably be heard all over the school.

"Oh my gosh," I said, and brought my hand up to my forehead. It throbbed, and from the way that Beck was rubbing his, I could tell he felt the same.

"Are you okay?" he asked, and I nodded, even though it felt like my forehead had been run over by a big truck. The warning bell rang, and I knew we needed to do this now or we'd be late for class.

"How about I wait until you lean forward," I said, remembering all the reality TV that Lizzie made me watch. The woman was always waiting for the man to move in for the kiss, and now I understood why.

"Good plan," Beck said. He kept his eyes open, but I closed mine and tried to pretend we were somewhere else, like at the beach or on a Ferris wheel. Somewhere other than this dark, dusty corner of the theater. I could feel his breath on my face and smell the mint he chomped minutes ago. My heart raced. This was it. I leaned the rest of the way and suddenly all the lights backstage went on.

"What are you two doing?" a voice yelled, and I jumped back so fast, I knocked all of Beck's supplies off the prop shelf.

It was Mr. O'Malley.

Our principal.

And about twenty other kids standing behind him.

Please tell me this isn't real. Please, please, please. I closed my eyes as if I could pretend this wasn't happening, but a loud voice forced me to open them.

"They were kissing," Bobby Kuhn said. Bobby was the most obnoxious boy in our grade and the last person in the world you'd want to find you when you were about to get your first kiss. Well, that and the crowd that was around him.

"We weren't kissing," I said quietly, because technically we hadn't kissed yet, and I couldn't think of what else to say.

"Mrs. Moran's English class is using the theater today to act out a scene from *Romeo and Juliet*," Mr. O'Malley said, all scary and stern despite the yellow smiley-face tie he wore. I focused on it while he talked so I didn't have to make eye contact with the group of kids who were focused on the two of us. "You, on the other hand, are not supposed to be anywhere near the theater alone."

I wanted to disappear. Instead, I stood frozen to the spot. I couldn't move. There was no hope, so I waited for Beck to say something to help us out, but he looked as scared as me. His eyes were wide and he played with the string that hung down from his hoodie.

And then he did the worst thing possible. He told the truth.

"I was helping Grace out. She needed me to kiss her."

Oh my gosh, I thought. *This is not happening. No, no, no.*

"To kiss her?" Mr. O'Malley asked, but I didn't wait to hear anything more because I did the second-worst thing possible.

I turned around and bolted.

I made my way out of the theater and down the hall as fast as I could. I didn't stop moving until I ran smack into James.

CHAPTER
Thirteen

"WHOA," JAMES SAID, PUTTING HIS HAND on my shoulder. I tried to push past him, football-player style, but he wouldn't let me. The boy was strong. He loosened his grip once I stopped struggling. How in the world did he end up being the first person I ran into?

He held up a pink tardy slip and waved it in my face. "Did you oversleep too?"

"I was in the theater. I didn't hear the bell ring," I said, trying to speak coherently, but my mind was spinning. Why did I place myself at the scene of the crime so easily? Why didn't I tell him I missed the bus and was racing to get to class on time, or was running to a study session, or chasing down a bully who stole a little kid's lunch money? There were a million good excuses I could have picked, and instead I went straight to the truth. Yeah, not bright at all.

"Oh, I know why you were in the theater," he said with a smirk.

He knew, I thought, my stomach twisting up in knots. Somehow he had already heard what happened. Gossip spread like wildfire around Sloane Middle School, and I bet everyone was already talking about it. I wanted to disappear, never to be seen or heard from again.

James wagged his finger as if I had done something bad. "Are you trying to show the rest of us up? Are you rehearsing in the morning too?"

I seized the opportunity to save myself and went with it. "Yes, yes, that's what I was doing. I was walking through the blocking for the scene when I first meet the dwarfs. There's too many of them, and I always end up moving the wrong way and running into someone."

"You should have told me you needed someone to rehearse with. I would have helped you." He pulled his script out of his backpack. "I've been trying to memorize my lines for the last few days and would love a partner to work with."

"Really?" I asked. James wanted to practice with me? I

assumed he ran lines with the other eighth graders in the show. People like Michelle and her awful friends. Those girls made sure to give me a hard time whenever they were able to. More often than not, when I messed something up, moved the wrong way, or forgot to do something, they were there, whispering and making comments under their breath. Michelle didn't need to rehearse her role as the Evil Queen—she lived it every single day.

"Of course. I'm your Prince Charming," he said, and dipped down in a deep bow like he did in the show. "We need to help each other out. After all, without me you'd still be sleeping."

I closed my eyes and groaned. He'd brought up the kiss. Why, oh why, did he mention the kiss?

I blushed so red there was no way anyone could be calling this Snow White the fairest in the land. More like the brightest tomato in the land.

"Okay, well, I'd better get to class," James said, looking a little bit embarrassed too. "But maybe we could practice our lines sometime?"

"Sure, that would be cool," I said.

He turned and ran off down the hall, and I thought about how I had definitely not been cool.

CHAPTER
Fourteen

MR. O'MALLEY MADE ME SWEAT OUT MY punishment for the rest of the day as I went to all my classes. He didn't send for me until last period. The office slip came quietly, delivered by a redheaded boy I recognized from eighth grade. Mrs. Reichard stopped her lesson and gave him a dirty look for interrupting.

"You're wanted in the office, Grace," she said, and passed me the yellow piece of paper. "I'd suggest taking your stuff, since the school day is almost over."

I felt everyone's eyes on me as I slipped out the door as fast as possible so they couldn't see how bad my hands were shaking.

I walked slowly to the office, taking my sweet time, because why rush to your doom? Mr. O'Malley was a stickler for following rules and order; no one stepped out of place with him. Once, he gave Lizzie a detention for throwing a grape, but the thing was, she didn't even do it. She was trying to eat one and it slipped out of her hand. A three-hour detention! The man was brutal!

I couldn't imagine what he had in store for Beck and me. He might have us scrub the bathroom floors with toothbrushes or scrape all the gum off the desks with our bare hands. Whatever it was, the punishment would be bad. I could feel it in my bones, kind of like how my grandpa used to say he could feel the rain coming in his creaky old knees. I hoped the two of us didn't have to do it together, because I was done with Beck for as long as I lived.

I made my way to the office and imagined myself walking to my untimely end, like a pirate forced to walk the plank, each step pulling me closer and closer to the loss of my freedom.

I gave my slip to the secretary; she nodded her head toward Mr. O'Malley's door, which was shut.

"Go ahead in, Grace. They're both there. Mr. O'Malley's already talked to him alone and now they're waiting for you."

I looked up to the ceiling and groaned. Beck was in there

too? This wasn't the way this day was supposed to turn out. If I had to get in trouble, the least I could have gotten out of it was that stupid kiss. But no, oh no. I pushed the door open slowly. *There'd better be two chairs far, far away from each other, because I am not going to sit anywhere near Beck.*

But when I walked in, the chairs weren't what I focused on. It was who was in one of the chairs that made me stop dead in my tracks. Beck wasn't the one sitting with Mr. O'Malley.

It was Dad.

CHAPTER
Fifteen

MR. O'MALLEY SAT BEHIND HIS DESK, HIS smiley-face tie pressed up against the edge as he leaned forward. There were two chairs across from him. I sat down in the chair next to Dad without saying a word. This was now a very big deal. Dad was missing work, which meant someone else was doing the twenty-second weather updates that aired at half past the hour until the evening news came on. If the day's theme was kissing, I was about to kiss my freedom good-bye.

I didn't dare look at either of them, because if I did, I'd cry. It was taking every ounce of willpower right now not to, and the last thing I wanted to do was cry in front of Dad.

Instead, I checked out Mr. O'Malley's office. I had never been in the principal's office before, and I was surprised at how calming it was. The walls were painted a pale blue, the chairs were soft and cushy, and his desk was lined with pictures of his family. When I'd thought about what his office would be like, I'd envisioned something a lot worse. Maybe he would have those medieval torture devices we learned about in history, the ones that pulled your fingernails off and let single drops of water fall on your forehead for hours. Or posters of the most wanted students, like the ones I see of fugitives on the run when I go with Mom to the post office. Going to the principal's office always seemed so scary, and I was glad the room didn't live up to my expectations.

"Grace, you understand why your father is here, right?" Mr. O'Malley asked. I stalled. He probably thought I was going through the millions of reasons why I might have gotten in trouble and needed my dad to come in, but what I wanted to tell him was that I wasn't that type of person. I wasn't a girl who got in trouble; this was all a big mistake.

Instead, I tried to appear very, very sorry. I pushed my lower lip out a bit and gave him my best puppy-dog eyes. The same ones I practiced in front of the mirror when I tried to convince Mom to buy me a cell phone. It never worked with her, but maybe Mr. O'Malley would buy it. "Yes, and I know what I did was wrong."

"Do you?" he asked, and I wished he hadn't chosen that tie today. There wasn't anything cheerful about the situation, and it was as if all those little yellow faces were laughing at me.

I nodded, and tried to think about happy things—puppies, summer vacation, ice cream—anything to keep the tears away.

"I've explained to your father what happened, so I don't think we need to go back over it again. But what we need to make clear is that there are certain spots in the school you're not supposed to be in without a teacher, and the theater is one of them. You know this. Your teachers go over the rules the first day of school. I wouldn't have called your father if this was only about your being in a restricted area, but the fact that you were with a boy makes this more serious, and more serious for Beck, too."

I glanced at Dad and squirmed in my seat. Did Mr. O'Malley have to stress that I was with a boy? It was bad enough Dad was here, but to repeat that made it so much worse. I hoped Beck wouldn't get off any easier. He deserved to squirm too.

"You're a good student, Grace. I'm surprised to have you in here. And I'm surprised to have to talk to Beck as well."

"I still *am* a good student," I told him, and the tears did start. They rolled down my face in fat, wet blobs. I wiped them away, but more appeared.

"Honey," Dad spoke up, "we know that you are, but do you understand that there are reasons why people make rules? You can't choose which to follow and which not to."

I scrunched down in my seat and tried to pretend I was invisible.

"We're not trying to make you feel bad," Mr. O'Malley said, his stern tone softening a bit. I felt as if the two of them were ganging up on me, and I needed to get out of there. "I want to make sure you're going to make the right choices from now on, correct?"

"Oh yes, sir, yes," I said shaking my head up and down to confirm it. I felt like a human bobblehead. At this point I would have done anything to get out of Mr. O'Malley's office.

"Good, this conversation is over. Since there's only about ten minutes left to the day, why don't you go ahead home with your father." Mr. O'Malley stood up and walked around the desk to Dad. "Thanks for taking the time to come in, Chris."

"Of course, and I'll make sure Grace doesn't do this again," Dad said, and suddenly he didn't seem as kind as he did a moment ago when I was upset. It sounded like Dad intended to give me a second round of lecturing and I would be trapped in the car during it all.

Dad shook Mr. O'Malley's hand, and then I did too. I held it tight and didn't let go when I felt his hand loosen. *Keep me in here*, I said in my head, and tried to send the vibes to Mr. O'Malley. He gave me a funny look and pulled his hand back slightly. *Great. Now he probably thinks I'm some creep girl who tried to hold his hand*. I slunk out after Dad, not looking at anyone. Especially not the secretary, who was probably eager to hear what happened to the girl who made the boy kiss her backstage.

The embarrassment didn't end when we walked out of the office. Of course it didn't; the day just kept getting worse, because sitting outside on the chairs next to Mr. O'Malley's office was the last person I wanted to see right now.

Beck.

He was there with his parents, no doubt about to get the same talking-to by Mr. O'Malley. His dad was paging through a pile of papers on his lap and his mom had her hand on Beck's shoulder, as if he were going to jump up and leave. Beck looked about as miserable as I was.

Dad nodded at the three of them, but I refused to make

eye contact. I followed Dad out of the school. Two girls slowed down when I passed and giggled, and a boy wiggled his eyebrows at me. Oh no! They knew. The word had spread.

I glanced at Dad, but he hadn't noticed. He was too busy typing away on his phone, and I prayed it wasn't a message to Mom.

CHAPTER
Sixteen

DAD DIDN'T SAY A WORD ONCE WE GOT into the car, which was quite all right with me. I pretended things were perfectly fine and he was only giving me a ride home. Well, at least I did until we made it to the turn for our street and he kept on going.

"Um . . . do you know we passed our street?" I asked. Dad had been gone for a long time, but not long enough to forget where he lived.

"There's a storm coming this afternoon, so I thought we'd go to the lake."

As Dad drove the rest of the way, I remembered all the trips we used to make to Lake Erie. It was at the tip of our town. It reached all the way to Canada, and when I was young I stood on the shore and pretended I could see the people on the other side. It used to be one of my favorite places to go with Dad. We'd sit on one of the benches that faced the water and watch the weather roll in. Dad would make sure something cool was going on: a meteor shower, the potential for a rainbow, winds so strong the waves would grow tall and rough so it looked as if we lived on the ocean.

Today I could tell it would be storm gazing. The sky was heavy with clouds and a wind whipped around us as we got out of the car and walked toward the water. Dad knew exactly when a storm would reach shore, which also meant he knew exactly when we should leave the beach so we wouldn't get drenched.

"We haven't done this in a while, have we?" he said once we sat down.

"Nope." The wind pulled my hair all over the place and the waves slammed against the rocks below. Dad kept his eyes on the horizon, and I studied my green shoes as if they were the most fascinating things in the world. This morning, when Dad had helped me pick them out, seemed so long ago. It felt as if I'd dreamed the nervous excitement at the start of my day and the reality had turned into a nightmare.

89

"One time the station made me do a report from here and the weather was so bad, it knocked the cameraman over. The two of us could hardly stay standing, but they made me keep reporting." He laughed softly and stared out over the water.

I wanted to tell him that I remembered a lot of things about this lake. Like the time our family packed a picnic lunch, and when we came back from playing on the playground near the parking lot, someone's dog was sitting on our blanket, chewing on Mom's peanut butter and jelly sandwiches. Or the time Dad took us all to watch the sunrise, but it was too cloudy and we couldn't see anything. The lake used to be our special place, and I wondered if Dad thought about all the things we did here as clearly as I did.

"Sooooo," Dad said, stretching the word out to make it sound a lot longer than one syllable. "Do you want to tell me why you and Beck were backstage?"

"Not really," I told him. I watched the sky light up as the storm hovered far out over the water. The bellies of the clouds lit up bright white and dimmed back to gray.

Dad shifted and the bench creaked. "I think we should talk about this."

"I don't," I mumbled, and squirmed in my seat, but he

wasn't going to let me off the hook. I could sulk all I wanted to, but Dad was the master of waiting things out.

"How about we try?" he asked.

I snuck a look at him out of the corner of my eye. He was tapping his fingers against his knee in the way he does when he's nervous, and he seemed as uncomfortable as I was to be having this conversation.

I shrugged and tried to act like it wasn't a big deal. "It was a mistake," I said, and wished this conversation could end right now. This was not what I wanted to talk to Dad about. Dad and I didn't have conversations like this. Heck, we hadn't had any sort of conversation in months.

"Mistake or not, you shouldn't have been there," Dad said.

"It won't happen again," I said to get him to stop talking about this with me. "Lizzie was the one who talked us into doing it."

"Lizzie talked you into kissing Beck?" Dad sighed loudly. "Grace, you're smarter than that. Do I need to worry about you letting your friends convince you to do things you don't want to?"

I closed my eyes and rubbed my temples like I'd seen Mom do when she got a headache. How did things suddenly get to this point? Now Dad was about to give me a talk about peer pressure. If I didn't set him straight, he'd use the good old friend-jumping-off-a-bridge analogy. He was as bad as Mom about these things.

"Lizzie didn't talk me into kissing him," I told him a little too loudly. A girl pushing a child in a stroller in front of us paused and glanced our way. I lowered my voice. "It wasn't her fault."

"Well, if she didn't, then who did?" Dad asked in his tone of voice that reminded me a lot of the old Dad. The one who would yell when Claire and I were fighting over something stupid at dinner or who busted into my room and told me to take my clothes out of the dryer and fold them when I forgot, even after Mom told me a million times. This version of Dad meant business. He wasn't going to leave me alone until I explained myself, so I tried the best I could without sounding as pathetic as I knew the situation was.

"I was the one who wanted to kiss him," I said quietly, pretty much dying from embarrassment. "Snow White gets kissed in the play. I've never kissed anyone before. Beck was helping me practice as a friend. It won't happen again, so can we please stop talking?"

I kept my eyes forward, on the sky. It was getting darker out and pretty soon the rain would reach us. I felt Dad shift toward me and his hand went to my shoulder.

"Growing up is hard, huh, kiddo?"

"Yeah," I said, and my voice caught in my throat in that pitiful, sniffling way. I wanted the conversation to be over, and it seemed to be, but there was one more thing I needed to ask Dad. It was awful that he showed up at school, there's no denying that, but it would be nothing compared to Mom's reaction when she heard about what happened. She had this way of overreacting to little things, like the time she found out I'd skipped my piano lessons and walked to the ice cream store with Lizzie. She made me practice piano for an hour every night for two weeks straight. Or the time I broke her hair dryer and blamed it on Claire. Mom made me wash dishes until I earned back enough money to pay for a new one because I lied about my sister breaking it. There was no way she'd let this one slide.

I pulled my lucky marble out of my pocket and rolled it around in the palm of my hand. I took a deep breath. *Here goes nothing.*

"Do you have to tell Mom?"

Dad ran his hand through his hair and let out another big sigh. It was as if he knew I was going to ask him this question. "She's your mother. I think we should tell her."

"She'll go nuts over this. Please. You know how she is.

She'll make me quit the play." This was probably true. Mom was all about Claire or me learning our lesson when we did something wrong, and what better way to teach me than to take away the thing I loved most?

Dad didn't know what to do. He chewed on his lower lip and seemed to be lost in thought. He needed to agree to be quiet about this; I couldn't lose the play.

"Please," I said as a crackle of thunder cut through the air. The sky was almost black and the wind had picked up even more. "Please, please, please."

Dad watched the water, thinking through things. Finally he nodded. "Okay, just this once. We'll keep it between us. But," he said, and held up his finger, "if I hear about anything like this happening again, all bets are off. Do you understand?"

"Yes, sir," I said.

"Calling me Dad would be a lot better," he said, sounding sad. There was some truth in his words. I hadn't called him Dad since he came home. In fact, it had been a long, long time since I'd thought of him as my dad and not someone who had turned his back on us and walked out.

"Okay, Dad," I said softly, the word sounding strange but familiar at the same time.

CHAPTER
Seventeen

WHEN DAD AND I GOT HOME, I TOLD MOM I was going to take a nap and stayed upstairs until she called me back down to eat. During dinner I shoveled in the food as fast as I could because I was afraid Dad would say something about this afternoon.

"How about after dinner you call Beck," Mom said in between bites of chicken casserole. "He called twice when you were upstairs. I told him you were taking a nap, but he called back ten minutes ago, checking to see if you were awake yet."

"I don't feel like talking to him right now," I said with a little too much force in my voice.

"You always want to talk to Beck," Mom said, and eyed me suspiciously.

"Not anymore. The next time he calls, tell him I never want to hear his voice again. On second thought . . ." I got up and walked over to the phone. I unplugged the cord so he couldn't get through even if he wanted to. "Let's give the phone a rest for the night."

"What did he do to make you so mad?" Mom asked as she walked over to the phone and put the cord back in. "I thought you two were good friends."

"Believe me, you don't want to know," I said, and ate the rest of my meal quickly. I excused myself from the table and headed to my room to see if Lizzie wanted to talk on the walkie-talkies, even though she'd probably only want to talk about kissing some more. On my way there, I glanced out our front window and saw Evan. He was walking down his driveway with his big yellow Lab, Rascal.

Suddenly, fresh air sounded really good right about now. And before I knew it, I'd grabbed Darby's leash and clicked it on his collar.

"I'm taking Darby for a walk around the block," I yelled, and pulled him out the door before anyone could respond. We lived on a quiet side street, and usually my parents were okay with me taking Darby for a walk at night, but I didn't want to risk it. I ran down the front walk to make sure neither of them would stop me, or worse, want to come along.

Darby yanked me down the front yard to his favorite spot under the apple tree. As he sniffed around I thought about what just happened. Why had I raced outside after Evan? We hadn't talked since that morning at the bus stop, and he might think it was weird that I suddenly appeared outside with my dog. But I felt like he kind of got me. In a way that Lizzie and my parents couldn't right now.

It didn't matter what my reason was, though, because he wasn't around anymore. I took my time anyway; staying outside in the quiet was a lot better than trying to act as if everything inside was normal. I let Darby do his thing, which meant smell every single tree and hydrate every blade of grass in our yard. He moved at a snail's pace, his nose stuck to the ground, his black tail wagging back and forth. I had no idea what he was smelling, but he sure was happy about it. I wished I could find something that made me that happy. If someone had asked me five days ago, I would have said it was the play, but even that gave me nothing but a sick feeling in my stomach when I thought about that kiss.

"Full moon tonight," a voice said behind me.

I jumped, startled, and then calmed down a bit when I saw it was Evan coming from his backyard with his dog. So he was still outside. Darby wiggled around and wagged his tail, and for some reason, I felt as if I'd be doing the same if I could.

"It's a good night for werewolves," I told him, and grinned.

"What if one sneaks up on you?"

"I have Darby to guard me." I pointed down to my attack dog, who had decided it was a pretty good time to lie down on his side. He thumped his tail but made no move to stand up. "Okay, maybe I wouldn't make it out alive against a werewolf attack."

"We were about to head out for a walk," Evan said, and bent down to pet Rascal.

"Same here." I chewed on my bottom lip. I didn't know why I suddenly felt nervous. I hung out with Beck, who was a boy, all the time and it never felt weird. But with Evan, it seemed . . . different. But good different. I decided to take a risk. Before I could stop myself, I asked, "Want to come with us?"

"Sure. Which direction were you heading?" Evan asked, and I pointed to the right.

Darby got up and walked a few feet ahead of us, happily smelling anything that Rascal stopped and sniffed at. Evan and

I quickly fell into step beside each other and didn't say anything for a little bit. The dogs huffed and puffed as they strained to walk faster, filling the silence between the two of us.

Evan leaned against a tree and faced me when the dogs stopped to sniff a smell so great, their tails wagged. "How are things at your school?"

"Fine," I said, and pushed away all thoughts about this morning. I wasn't about to spill those to Evan.

"Just fine? I heard something pretty exciting happened there," he said, and I froze. He knew. The news about what happened today had jumped from Sloane Middle School and invaded Lakewood Academy. Maybe the whole city was laughing right now about what had happened in the theater. Darby tugged on my leash, wanting to move forward.

"Nope. Same old, same old," I said quickly.

"My mom said you got the lead in the school play," Evan said, and my whole body relaxed.

Phew! "Yep, Snow White."

"You must be so excited."

"It's pretty cool," I said, but the usual roller-coaster feeling filled my stomach as I thought about the kiss. I changed the subject so we were talking about him. "How about you? How's your grandma?"

"Not so great. She fell and now has to stay downstairs."

"I'm sorry," I said, because I didn't know what else to say.

Evan shrugged and bent down to pet Rascal. "My parents spent all of yesterday turning our dining room into a bedroom. Our table is shoved in a corner of our family room, next to our TV. Grandma hates it, and we have to walk around quietly when she's taking a nap."

"You could move into Claire's playhouse in our backyard," I told him. "That might be the most normal place these days."

"If you call not having a bathroom or electricity normal."

I laughed, both at that comment and the fact that we were now talking about bathrooms.

"What about you?" Evan asked. "How are things with your dad?"

"Hard," I said, and waited for Evan to change the subject or ignore me like Lizzie did. Except, he didn't.

"I totally get that. Sometimes I wish my grandma wasn't staying with us," he said, and I knew just what he meant. "I want things to feel normal again."

"That's exactly how I feel," I whispered. "But I don't even know what normal is anymore."

Neither of us said anything, and we continued on our walk in silence until Evan stopped. We were almost back home, but he froze and put a finger up to his lips to get me to stay quiet. He pointed across the yard: there were four deer standing right in a huge patch of moonlight. One of them was a buck with antlers that stretched farther than both my arms opened wide. We stood side by side, our shoulders touching, and watched them, neither of us making a move to leave or scare them away. I didn't dare move, and I wasn't quite sure if it was because of the deer or Evan.

Darby finally got tired of sniffing the grass in front of him and lifted his head in the air, spotting the deer. He barked, which got Rascal's attention and startled the animals. The deer ran away and Darby lunged after them. His leash flew out of my hand and he was off.

"Shoot," I said. "Grab him!"

The two of us and Rascal sprinted after Darby, who now ran around and around in a circle where the deer had been seconds ago. When I caught up with him, I stepped on his trailing leash and grabbed hold of him again. Darby jumped up on me and knocked me into Evan like a bowling ball hitting a pin. We were pulled to the ground and lay in a heap. Darby finally gave up the fight and collapsed beside us on the grass, panting. Rascal sat near him, as if amused by everything that had just happened.

"Got him?" Evan asked, and I nodded. I could feel his heart beating underneath my arm. The hair on my arm prickled and I tried to calm my breathing.

Evan was the first one to move, and when he got up, he offered his hand to me. I took it and my stomach flipped over and over in a fluttery dance. He let go once I was up, and we walked back to our houses not saying much, but maybe that was a good thing, because all I could think about was how fast Evan's heart was beating, and the feel of his hand in mine. It was weird. Usually I was so nervous around boys, but with Evan it felt different. I liked spending time with him, and I hoped he felt the same way.

CHAPTER
Eighteen

BECK'S APOLOGY CAME IN THE FORM OF apples.

Bright red, shiny apples.

He left them everywhere—in front of my locker, on my desk during math class—and even got an office messenger to deliver a bag to me during English. When I went home there would probably be crates of them in front of my house. Maybe I could talk Mom into making an apple pie or apple crisp, although there were probably enough apples to make pies and crisps for my entire grade. But baking wasn't what Beck had in mind with the apples: he wanted me to forgive him.

"Beck gave you all of these?" Lizzie asked, confused when

I dumped a new bag into my locker. There were only so many apples a person could lug around.

"He's nuts," I said. From my pocket I pulled out the note that came with the first batch and passed it to her. I'd read it enough times that I knew the words by heart.

"'To my good friend, Grace,'" Lizzie read out loud, and I rolled my eyes. "'I'm so sorry for what I said backstage yesterday. It was very, very wrong of me. I know you are mad, but I would bite into a million poisonous apples and fall asleep forever if it meant you would forgive me. From your very sorry friend, Beck.'"

"I'm ready to send them all back and tell him to start chewing," I told Lizzie.

She handed the note to me and shrugged. "You have to admit, it's pretty sweet. He's trying to make things better."

"Well, he needs to try harder, because I don't think there's anything he can do to make up for ruining my entire life."

"Your life isn't ruined. No one even mentioned it today. You're the only one who remembers. We've moved on. There's too much other juicy gossip to talk about."

Lizzie was right about that. Aside from a few stray comments here and there, and one awful incident in English class where someone passed me a fake ticket sloppily drawn and labeled *Admit one person to Sloane Middle School's Backstage Kissing Extravaganza*, what happened yesterday was old news. Especially after Sharon Lazzaro walked around for a good ten minutes with her skirt tucked into her tights.

"What are you going to do this afternoon at rehearsal? You'll have to talk to him at some point. You can't run away every time you see him."

"Why not? It's worked so far." But Lizzie was right: I couldn't keep turning around when I spotted Beck in the hallway. Eventually he was going to catch up with me, but today there were bigger things to deal with. We were almost done blocking all the scenes in the play, which meant that soon— very, very soon—it would be time for the kiss. Mrs. Hiser scheduled that scene for next Tuesday, and the day that once seemed so far away seemed way too close now.

CHAPTER
Nineteen

I COLLECTED MORE APPLES AS THE DAY went on, but still refused to talk to Beck. Although Lizzie was right: when it was time for rehearsal, I didn't know where to sit.

There was no way I could join Michelle's group, and on the other side of the room, Lizzie made sure to plant herself down next to Beck. She gestured at me to sit near them, but I wouldn't fall for her trap; she couldn't force me to sit next to Beck. Instead, I took a seat by some kids who were part of the ensemble. Thankfully, Mrs. Hiser arrived soon after and called for everyone's attention.

"All right, let's begin. Do we have everyone here?"

Michelle caught my eye, smiled, and raised her hand.

"Mrs. Hiser, I think we're missing Grace and Beck. Maybe we should check backstage in the prop corner."

The room erupted in laughter, and I willed the floor to open up and swallow me whole. I couldn't believe Michelle had said that.

"That's enough," Mrs. Hiser snapped. She frowned at Michelle. Mrs. Hiser rarely got mad, and when she did, you knew she was serious. The cast got quiet and watched to see if Michelle would react. She kept her head down and dug around in her bag, and Mrs. Hiser refocused on the rehearsal. "Much better. Today I planned to work on blocking the scene we scheduled with the dwarfs, but we're missing two of them, and we can't have Snow White with only five dwarfs. So we're going to skip ahead to the last scene, which features most of the cast. We'll be able to catch up with the two missing dwarfs a lot easier."

My heart stopped. No lie. It felt like it stopped beating for a good ten seconds or more. The last scene was the kissing scene. *No, no, no, not today,* I thought. This was not supposed to happen. I stood up, thinking of nothing but the fact that I needed to stop what was about to happen.

"Wait, I thought we weren't doing the ending until next week," I shouted out, sounding like a complete idiot.

"Is there a problem with moving ahead?" Mrs. Hiser asked.

"Um, no, sorry. I was trying to memorize my lines, and I haven't gotten there yet." I tried to sound normal when all I wanted to do was puke my guts out. *Please let this be a bad dream.* I pinched myself hard, but all I got was a big red mark on my skin and a lot of pain. This was indeed real.

Michelle snorted and mimicked me in a high-pitched voice. *"I was trying to learn my lines."*

A bunch of people laughed, and I put my hands on my hips and faced her. Hot anger flashed through me. She wasn't going to embarrass me for a second time today. I was sick of her acting as if she owned the place. "What's the matter with trying to memorize my lines?"

"Yeah, it's a lot harder for Grace to learn her lines than it is for you," Beck spoke up. "She has at least five times the lines you have, and I don't see you going off-book yet."

I tried to keep a smile off my face, but I couldn't. Leave it to Beck to lay another one of his burns on Michelle. Even when I was mad at him, he was still awesome.

Michelle sat back on the couch, her lips pursed. I could practically see her plotting horrible revenge in her mind.

"Since we're doing the last scene, those of you who are involved with the queen and her castle workers can leave,"

Mrs. Hiser said, and made it a point to look at Michelle. "We'll go over the scene we skipped next week, on the day we were supposed to be blocking this one."

I watched Michelle stand up. She gathered all her stuff, huffing and puffing the entire time. She didn't look at me again and left the room without saying good-bye to anyone.

"Good riddance, right?" Beck said in my ear. I didn't even notice him come over to me, but I wasn't about to let him see the satisfaction I was feeling about the way he put Michelle in her place.

I narrowed my eyes at him. "Sticking up for me doesn't mean I've forgiven you," I hissed.

"At least you're talking to me. I'll take that as a good sign," he said, but it wasn't with the usual energy that Beck had. He actually sounded a bit sad.

"I need to pay attention to what's going on," I said, and moved as far as I could from him. I listened as Mrs. Hiser put us into our places. I didn't dare look at James; I couldn't look at him.

I stepped into my spot to block the last scene. *I can do this,* I told myself. *I can be brave and face my fears.*

And that's just what I did for the first ten minutes. I was amazing. Well, as amazing as you can be when all you have to do is lie flat and pretend to sleep while a bunch of forest animals and dwarfs sob around you. I was amazing right up to the point where James leaned over to wake me up with a single kiss.

Be brave, be brave, be brave, I chanted in my mind. I repeated my mantra over and over again as I felt James get ready for the big kiss, and I really, honestly thought I would go through with it, but then I couldn't.

I sat straight up like a zombie who had risen from the dead. It was so sudden that James jumped back and one of the dwarfs gasped.

"Ummm . . . ," I said, and stopped. Because what was I going to do? Admit to the entire room that I wasn't ready for my first kiss? James stared at me in confusion and Lizzie stood with her mouth wide open. Her eyes were huge, and I knew I had made a huge mistake.

"Are you okay?" Mrs. Hiser asked, stepping into the middle of everything.

I tried to think fast and blurted out the first excuse that kind of made sense. "My throat is on fire; I think I'm coming down with something. I don't want to pass it on to James."

I stopped babbling, and it felt as if someone hit the pause button on a movie. No one did anything for a moment. Then Mrs. Hiser nodded her head.

"I agree. This is a good stopping point for you, Grace. Rest up and make sure you're okay."

Mrs. Hiser bought it, hook, line, and sinker. In fact, it seemed as if the entire room had. Even James looked relieved. Great, he didn't even want to kiss me. He was probably glad I said I was feeling sick.

Mrs. Hiser clapped her hands together and got everyone's attention. "Let's work on the scene in the town square. If you're not in that scene, you can go home and work on getting your lines down. We're going off-book in two weeks, so be ready. I'm not throwing out lines for those of you who forget."

I followed some of the cast members away from the middle of the stage. There was no way I'd forget my lines, especially the scene we just went over. Those words were burned deep within my brain and turned me into a crazy person willing to make a fool out of herself every day.

James caught up with me on our way out. "Feel better," he said, and smiled so that his braces flashed in the lights.

"Thanks," I said, and tried to make my throat sound scratchy so he'd buy my lie. I was sick all right, but not with a sore throat. I was sick of being the girl who had the most confusing life in the world.

CHAPTER
Twenty

THANKFULLY, LIZZIE WAS AROUND LATER that night.

My walkie-talkie crackled to life and I tried to speak as calmly as one who almost had a major kissing emergency can. "Today was way too close."

"You should have gone for it. James was moving in for the kill before you jumped up and made an idiot of yourself."

"I couldn't," I moaned. I felt miserable about what had happened earlier today. "I thought I was brave enough to get through it, but I chickened out."

"Grace, the phrases 'brave enough' and 'get through it' should never be used when talking about kissing James."

"Don't remind me," I said, and planted my face in my pillow. I screamed as loud as I could, out of frustration. When I was done, I pushed the button on the side of the walkie-talkie again. "I need your help."

"You do?" Lizzie said with a bit of excitement in her voice.

"I'll do whatever I need to do," I said. "I need to get this kiss out of the way so I can stop worrying. I'm going to have an ulcer by the time this show is over." I wasn't even quite sure what an ulcer was, but when Uncle Tim got one, Mom and Dad said it was because of stress. All he did for weeks was chug milk to soothe what he says is the fire-breathing dragon in his stomach.

"I do have some ideas in mind, if you're willing to let me help you," Lizzie said, and I detected a hint of a laugh in her voice. This wasn't a laughing matter.

"I'll do anything," I pleaded.

"Okay, I'll brainstorm tonight and we'll talk about it at lunch tomorrow. The three of us."

"Oh no," I told her, understanding where she was headed with this one. "We're not bringing Beck into this."

"I refuse to divide my time between the two of you. The three of us are friends. You need to figure out how to fix things with him before lunch tomorrow or you're on your own with Operation Pucker Up."

"Yeah, sure, okay," I mumbled, because at this point I didn't have any other options. My time was running out. Today made that abundantly clear, and now I was racing the clock.

CHAPTER
Twenty-One

BECK WAS TAKING THIS *SNOW WHITE* thing way too far when he showed up at my locker the next morning with a mirror. He held it out in front of me so my face reflected back. I remembered what Lizzie had asked me to do last night, and I got rid of the angry-girl glare that stared back at me and tried to appear a little friendlier.

"You are the fairest in the land," Beck said, and pulled the mirror down so it was his face that I could now see. "And I shouldn't have said what I did backstage in the theater. It was wrong, and I was stupid."

"You're right. That was an awful thing to do," I told him. "And that line with the mirror, lame."

"I mean it, though, Grace. I'm sorry about what I said. It wasn't right to make you take the fall, and I told Mr. O'Malley that when he called my parents into his office to talk about what happened."

"You did?" I asked, surprised.

"I couldn't let you get in trouble. I'll tell Mrs. Moran's class too, if you want me to."

"You don't have to do that," I said. I knew Lizzie wanted me to make up with Beck, but I felt like it was important to let Beck know exactly what I went through. "It made me feel really stupid. What you did. Everyone thought I made you kiss me. It was beyond humiliating."

Beck bit his bottom lip and stared down at his shoes. When he raised his blue eyes back up to meet mine, I didn't feel the anger from the past few days. Instead, I saw my friend Beck with his wild curly hair and headphones that always hung around his shoulders. I saw the Beck who would compete with me to see who could drink their slushies the fastest before getting a brain freeze, and the Beck who never made fun of the fact that I didn't know how to whistle. I couldn't stay mad at Beck, especially now.

"I'll never do anything like that to you again," Beck said, and I wanted to believe him. I wanted to move on and have my friend back.

"Can we pretend the other morning never happened?" I asked.

"What morning?" Beck asked. "I don't know what you're talking about."

I grabbed Beck's mirror. I stood next to him and held it in front of us. "It looks good to have you back by my side."

"No two people ever looked better." Beck grinned, and I smiled back.

"I'll see you at lunch, because according to Lizzie, we have some plotting to do."

Beck's smile disappeared, and I couldn't help but laugh.

"Don't worry, I made it clear that her plans can't involve any dark spaces or early-morning theater classes."

Beck dropped his bag and wrapped his hands around me in a hug so tight that he then tried to pick me up. I kicked my legs and yelled for him to put me down.

"It's good to have you back," Beck said before heading off down the hallway with one last wave.

I turned back to my locker and dug though the mess, searching for the English paper I had shoved inside at some point. Lizzie called my locker the bottomless pit, and I couldn't argue with that one. I pushed aside old worksheets, candy wrappers, books, and tennis shoes and finally found it sticking out of a folder. I stood up and was smoothing it when I heard a weird hissing noise behind me.

I stood up and saw Michelle, Susan, and Katie.

"Yuck. I can smell your reptile breath from here," Michelle said, and wrinkled her nose.

"My what?" I asked, even though I had a sinking feeling about what they meant.

"It's obvious why James didn't kiss you at practice yesterday," she said. "He told everyone it was because he couldn't stand the smell coming out of your mouth."

"That's not true," I argued. "We didn't finish the scene because my throat was sore."

"Yep, it makes sense," Susan said. "Lizard breath will do that to you. Maybe you should ask your mom to buy some mouthwash today."

The three of them cracked up as if they had made the

funniest joke in the world while I stood there frozen, a sinking feeling in my stomach.

Before anyone could say anything else, the bell saved me. All the people in the halls scattered and disappeared until I was the only one left. Just my stinky breath and me, now late for class.

CHAPTER
Twenty-Two

LIZZIE WAVED ME OVER IMPATIENTLY when I entered the cafeteria.

"What took you so long?" she demanded. Beck stood next to her, and I thought about how much better it was to have the three of us together.

"Sorry, Mrs. Moran wanted to go over my English paper," I told her, but it wasn't the truth. I couldn't bring myself to admit that I was in the bathroom, trying to figure out if what Michelle and her friends had said was true. I cupped my hand around my mouth and tried to smell my breath over and over again, but all I could smell was the soap on my hands from washing them.

"We've been waiting forever for you to get here," Lizzie said. She grabbed my hand and led me over to a table that was far away from where we usually sat with a bunch of other theater kids.

"She's exaggerating. We got here five minutes ago," Beck whispered in my ear.

"The three of us have some very important work to do," Lizzie said, and took a seat straight across from me. She pulled a notebook with a picture of a kitten wearing a princess crown out of her bag.

"This is the important work we have to do?" I pointed to the cover. Beck made a snorting noise as he tried to hide his laughter.

Lizzie scowled at the two of us. She put her hand over the front of the notebook. "It's all I had that was blank. Besides, it's what's inside that matters."

I reached for it so I could see what was so great inside, but she pulled it back toward her. She grabbed Beck's plate of Tater Tots and set them in front of me.

"Let's get down to business. Pretend these two Tots are you and James."

"Can you talk a little quieter?" I asked. James was sitting a few tables over.

"Hear her out," Beck said. "I can't wait to see what she planned if she needs to use my Tater Tots to demonstrate it."

I turned back to Lizzie and the ridiculous point she was trying to make.

"Okay, so right now you're focused on this single Tot," Lizzie said, and pointed to the one that represented James. "And while it looks greasy and tasty, you need to remember you have a whole dish full of other ones that are just as good."

She stopped talking to check to see if I understood what she was trying to say. I didn't.

"That's your solution," she said. "You need to think about all the other Tater Tots."

"Um, what does this have to do with kissing?"

Lizzie looked at me as if I was completely stupid, which I really didn't think I was. She was the one using greasy lunchroom food to make some kind of point. She gestured at all of them. "These other Tater Tots are the boys in our grade. One of them is going to give you your first kiss."

"He will?" I asked, still not believing a word she was saying, because, really, who believes a person who plays with her food?

She pushed the notebook toward me. "Go ahead, check this out. I present to you the official version of Operation Pucker Up."

"The official version?" I asked, and Beck laughed real loud. Lizzie gave him a look so evil that it scared me.

I reached for the notebook and opened to the first page. Lizzie had drawn hearts all over and written a title in capital letters: WAYS TO GET GRACE HER FIRST KISS FAST, ASAP, NOW!!! The title was embarrassing enough, but what was in the rest of the notebook was even more incredible. I turned page after page of magazine cutouts of people kissing. She must have spent hours searching for pictures. She'd taped in all different types: adults, people my grandparents' age, kids, movie stars, even two dogs touching noses, which kind of confused me. But it was what followed on the pages after the pictures that made me stop and really question if Lizzie was sane or not.

"What is this list?" I asked.

She had used different-colored pens to write ideas down, making sure to dot every i with a heart.

Beck grabbed the notebook out of my hand and read out loud: "'Pretend to be drowning and need CPR; pay one of the boys in our grade to kiss Grace; play spin-the-bottle; watch romantic movies; do someone's homework in exchange for a kiss; trap someone's little brother so Grace can kiss him; build a kissing booth . . .'"

Thankfully, Lizzie yanked the book out of his hand and put me out of his misery.

"You want me to tackle someone's little brother so I can get a kiss?" I asked, my voice rising so I sounded hysterical. "You're dreaming if you think I'm going to go through with this."

"Maybe some of these are a little far-fetched," Lizzie said, and I thought about telling her that "a little" was putting it mildly. "But I was only brainstorming ideas. We don't have to use them all. There are so many other people you can kiss and ways that we can make it happen."

"What if something goes wrong again?" I said, thinking about the history lesson from the other day about cowboys. I pictured myself with a bandanna around my face and a trusty steed, riding up to unsuspecting boys and stealing kisses.

"We won't get people to *agree* to kiss you, we'll put you in situations where people *want* to kiss you. I have a list of a whole bunch of different ideas in the notebook. It's foolproof. It will happen, and then you'll be able to relax and enjoy kissing that boy over there." Lizzie pointed her finger at James. He saw us staring at him and gave a little wave, his face breaking into a smile. He certainly didn't act like a boy who believed I had lizard breath.

"See?" Lizzie said, nudging me from under the table. "You

totally want to do this. We need to get you that kiss before it's too late."

I snuck another glance at James, who was still watching me, and my face heated up. I turned back to Lizzie and Beck. "Fine, but it's on my terms. If I don't want to do one of your ideas, I don't do it."

"Works for me," Lizzie said, but I wasn't so sure I trusted the smug look on her face, especially when she opened a new page in the notebook and rapidly wrote something down. It seemed as if Act Two was starting, and I wondered if this play had a happy ending.

CHAPTER
Twenty-Three

DAD WAS IN THE DRIVEWAY WHEN I GOT off the bus at the end of the day. The trunk of his big silver car was open and he carried a bunch of clothes on hangers. My heart dropped and I felt all dizzy, like I couldn't stand up any longer. I had seen this before, and it could only mean one thing.

"You're leaving again?" I asked softly, because sometimes it was easier to say the hard things quietly. When you spoke them loud enough that everyone could hear, it seemed so much more real. I couldn't believe it. How could he do this again? Had we done something wrong?

"Oh, honey, no," Dad said. He put the shirts down and

rushed over to me. He wrapped his arms around me and I pulled away at first, but then fit myself into him. The hug was both comfortable and unfamiliar at the same time. I tried hard to remember what it felt like to hug him and feel nothing but love and security. He finally pulled away and stooped down so we were on the same level. "I'm moving out of my apartment. The lease is up, and I need to empty the place out of all my stuff. That's what these shirts are."

"When I saw you with all your stuff, I thought . . ." I felt my throat clench up and stared up at the sky. I watched a bird do circles over the trees. I didn't want him to see that I was about to cry. I needed to be strong for Mom and Claire. I needed him to understand he couldn't do things like this to us.

Dad bent down in front of me so he was at my level. "Grace, I'm not going anywhere," he said, his voice taking on the serious tone he used to use when he and Mom would have their late-night talks. Conversations that were only murmurs from their bedroom, their voices rising and falling. In the beginning, I'd knock on their door and ask if everything was okay. That was before I learned things were not okay at all, even if Mom and Dad smiled and said they were.

"Please don't leave us again," I told him.

"I'm here to stay. You don't need to worry about that anymore."

"I want to believe you," I said. "But it's so hard."

I watched as Dad's eyes lost their brightness and filled with sadness. He wrapped his arms around me again, and I held on to him with all my might. I hoped he was telling the truth, and not just for Mom and Claire, but for me, too.

CHAPTER
Twenty-Four

DAD LEFT TO MAKE ANOTHER TRIP TO his old apartment but assured me over and over again that he was coming back, and I was glad he understood why I got so upset.

I really was trying to get used to having Dad back, but it seemed as if every time I got comfortable, I'd remember the things he missed in our lives when he left. How he wasn't sitting with us when I blew out the candles on my birthday cake or how he didn't go to the game where Claire scored her first soccer goal ever. It was as if I wanted him to be back in my life again, but I was too scared to let that happen. I didn't want to get disappointed, even if life was starting to feel a bit like normal again. And if I was truthful with myself, I liked having Dad back in the house. It felt good to hear him checking the locks on the doors at night or to see he'd whipped up a batch of his famous peanut butter chocolate chip cookies, the ones Mom hated because of all the sugar in them. I liked how the house smelled like coffee again and how basketball was the background noise on the TV more often than not. After so many months of living in a house where one of the most important things in it was missing, there was something good about living a life that felt whole again.

The phone rang twice while I was stuffing my face with some of the Oreos that Dad had smuggled home.

I ran upstairs and Lizzie spoke as soon as I turned on my walkie-talkie.

"Hey," I said, glad that I could talk to someone about what had happened. Mom wouldn't be home until later, and she'd be too busy trying to get Claire to finish up her homework and take a bath than to listen to me. "You won't believe what Dad was doing when I got home from school."

"Never mind that," Lizzie said in a rushed voice. "I have news. Round two of Operation Pucker Up goes into action on Saturday."

I closed my eyes and counted to ten until I calmed down.

It was something Mom always said she did when her nursing job got too crazy. Why couldn't Lizzie stop and listen to me for once? "I don't want to talk about Operation Pucker Up right now. I need to talk to someone about my dad."

"Grace, this is major. My neighbor Tricia came over to drop off some mail that got delivered to their house by accident and she told me she's having a birthday party."

I sighed loudly. There was no use trying to talk to Lizzie about important things when she got like this. Everything I said was going in one ear and out the other.

"And guess what? You get to be my plus-one!"

"Plus-one?" I asked, not sure what that meant, but if Lizzie had anything to do with it, I was sure it was something that would get me into trouble.

"My date. She said I could bring someone, so I choose you."

"Gee, thanks, but what's so great about a party full of girls we don't know?" Tricia went to the same private school Evan went to, which meant Lizzie and I would probably spend most of the time talking to each other. What did that have to do with Operation Pucker Up?

"Not just *girls*. Her mom is letting her invite boys, too. Cute boys, boys we haven't met yet, boys who would be perfect for you to practice your kissing on. It's the ideal setup, Grace." I

131

imagined her jumping around her room from excitement.

I did not like the sound of this at all. Sure, I'd been to parties with boys, but those were usually birthdays at the bowling alley or the pool parties where our parents stayed and chatted while we hung out. Parties where the boys were part of the fun, not what made the fun.

I knew Tricia from hanging out at Lizzie's house, and if there was ever a good example of boy crazy, she was it. "I don't think Tricia meant for you to bring another girl when she invited your plus-one."

"Well, she should have been more specific, because you're coming with me."

"My dad isn't going to let me go. Not after what happened at school in the theater. If he had his way, he'd be happy if I swore off boys until I was eighteen." I pulled back my window curtain and glanced at Evan's house. I wondered briefly if he was invited to the party too.

"We'll tell your parents you're hanging out at my house," Lizzie said. "You can get dropped off and picked up at my front door and it will be our little secret."

"I don't know," I said. I didn't want to press my luck. I was still scared that if Mom found out about what happened in the theater with Beck, she'd make me quit the play.

"Don't wimp out, Grace. There isn't a lot of time and this is the perfect place to practice your skills. You don't have to worry about if you're a bad kisser, because you'll never have to see them again."

She did have a point. The other day at rehearsal was too close for comfort. The kiss was coming soon, and if I didn't get some experience, I'd go down in history as the world's worst kisser when I finally did kiss James.

"Okay," I said. "I'll go for a little bit, but you have to promise not to ditch me. I won't know anyone there."

"You don't have to worry about that," Lizzie said. "But for the record, I wouldn't be mad if you ran off with some boy for a few kisses. Nope, I wouldn't be mad at all."

"That's not going to happen," I protested.

"Oh, don't be so sure of that. I have a feeling Operation Pucker Up is going to be a success. Now get some sleep, and I'll see you soon."

Lizzie signed off before I could bring Dad up again. I sighed and peeked out the window at Evan's house. I saw some movement in an upstairs window, a dark shadow that seemed to be standing behind the curtain. I wondered what Evan was doing, and if he worried about stupid things like first kisses, lizard breath, and not looking dumb in front of people.

 133

CHAPTER
Twenty-Five

LIZZIE WASN'T CONTENT TO FOCUS ONLY on the party. Of course not. Over the weekend, Lizzie tried to brainstorm other ways that could expedite my first liplock before the party. According to her, a lot could happen in the time between now and Tricia's big bash, and we shouldn't sit back and wait. Lizzie wanted to continue this torture as much as she could, which is why she begged me to go to her house for dinner after rehearsal on Monday. The plan was to do "field research," which meant observing her older sister and trying to figure out what exactly made Amy so popular with the boys. Amy's new boyfriend was coming over for dinner, and Lizzie thought it was the perfect opportunity to get some tips.

The two of us headed out of Lizzie's bedroom when her mom called us down to dinner, but I stopped in the doorway.

"You know, maybe the boys like her because she's pretty," I said, which was the truth. Amy's long blond hair was always perfectly wavy. Lizzie said she braided it at night before she went to bed, but I didn't believe it. Whenever I tried to do that with my own hair, it turned out to be a crazy ball of frizz.

"Ah, hello? . . . You're pretty too." Lizzie pushed me through the doorway into the hallway.

"Why are we bringing that with us?" I pointed at the Operation Pucker Up notebook she held in her hand. I didn't like the idea of her carrying it around. There was way too much information in there that could make me the talk of the school for life.

"We can write down everything we see Amy say or do that we think is 'important,'" Lizzie whispered as we walked down the stairs, even though everyone was in the dining room talking so loud they couldn't have heard us. Lizzie liked to make everything mysterious and full of the potential threat of danger.

"Or we could ask her," I suggested, although the thought of doing that embarrassed me.

"No way," Lizzie said. "We need to catch her being natural. Interacting with the male species."

"You make it sound as if this is some National Geographic special where the scientist goes into the animals' habitat to observe them."

"That's the idea. Picture our dining room table as the jungle."

I shook my head at Lizzie. There was no stopping her when she came up with a plan, regardless of how ridiculous it sounded.

"There's our Snow White," Mrs. Sheriban said when we got to the table. Lizzie's parents were there, along with Amy and her boyfriend, Adam. Her mom passed me a basket of rolls. "Are you ready for opening night?"

"Getting there," I told her.

"There are a few more important scenes she still needs to practice, but she'll be a pro by opening night," Lizzie said. I caught her eye and gave her a quick shake of the head to stop her from talking before she said too much.

"Ahh . . . it must be those dwarfs. Are they giving you trouble?" Mr. Sheriban asked as he loaded a big spoonful of mashed potatoes onto his plate.

"Something like that," I told him, not liking where this conversation was heading at all. Instead, I focused on Amy, who, according to Lizzie, represented what boys wanted.

I eyed her tight lace top skeptically. It stretched across her chest in a way that made me a little scared that if she bent over, stuff might fall out. I couldn't believe Lizzie's parents let her dress like that, especially since they were always making Lizzie wipe off the makeup she swiped from Amy and tried to wear to school.

"I heard that James Lowe is Prince Charming." Amy took a bite of her chicken. She wiped her lips with a napkin, and when she put it back down on the table, I could see splotches of her bright red lipstick. "His older brother is in my grade. Do good looks run in the family?"

"I haven't really thought about it," I said, playing dumb. "I'm too busy trying to learn my lines and make sure I don't mess up."

"Sure you haven't," Amy said, and gave me a look that made me feel as if she could see right into my brain and know exactly what I was thinking. She twirled a piece of her hair around and around her finger. I thought about picking up some of the mashed potatoes and flinging them at her to get her to be quiet. Luckily, Adam spoke up, so I didn't have to.

"What are you doing checking out other guys?" he asked, and slung his arm around her shoulder casually.

"I'm kidding," she said, and laughed in this obnoxious, high-pitched way. "You're my only Prince Charming."

She squeezed his shoulder and he looked content, even though I wanted to gag on the cheesiness of her line, especially since Adam seemed to be totally falling for it. He picked up her hand and held it right there at the table. I really hoped it wasn't because of her choice in clothing or the lame lines she was feeding him.

Lizzie was furiously scribbling in her notebook, no doubt recording all these interactions, none of which I planned to try out on any of the boys in my grade.

I watched everyone at the table talking, joking, and eating. Lizzie's dad told a story about one of his clients at the law firm he worked for, and I watched the way her mom sat with her cheek against her hand, leaning toward him and listening with a smile on her face. She interrupted a few times, and by the end of the story, the whole table was laughing so hard we had tears in the corners of our eyes. Lizzie's dad put his arm around her mom and pulled her toward him.

To everyone else at the table, what he did was nothing special. Lizzie kept right on scribbling words down, her sister flirted, and her dad talked. But for me, it made me think about how Mom and Dad used to be, before Dad worked late and missed dinners. We joked like that and the two of them seemed genuinely happy to be with each other. I wondered if there was a way my family could get that back. Things don't need to be lost forever, do they? Maybe it was time I tried trusting in what I had now instead of being afraid of what I would lose again. The fear I held inside when Dad first returned was slowly deflating out of me, and while it might not be easy to forgive Dad for what he did, maybe it was time I tried.

CHAPTER
Twenty-Six

LIZZIE DIDN'T SHARE HER NOTES WITH me after dinner that night. Instead, she said she wanted some time alone to review everything she wrote down and try to formulate a plan that was sure to get the attention of the boys at our school. I reminded her of the party coming up, but she said it was important to keep all our options open.

When she said "plan," I didn't know what to expect, but it certainly wasn't what she presented to me the next day.

She met me at my locker with a big duffel bag stuffed full.

"What's with all this stuff?" I asked as she dropped it in front of me. "Are you running away?"

"Funny," she said, and gave me a look that made it very

clear she didn't think I was funny at all. "This is part of Operation Pucker Up."

She reached into the bag and pulled out the notebook. She paged through it until she found the checklist and pointed at one of the lines.

"'Dress to wow the boys,'" I read aloud. I glanced down at my outfit. I wore a denim skirt with black tights and a long-sleeve pink top. I thought my choice of clothes was cute. "What's wrong with how I dress?"

"The outfit is good," Lizzie said, and took a step back to inspect me. "But you're missing a few important items. Things I noticed Amy wears all the time. Items that will help out your . . . *figure*."

She looked at me as if I knew what she meant, and if I was right about what she was thinking, I wished I didn't. I leaned against her locker and laughed nervously.

"My figure?" I glanced down at myself. I looked like a surfboard, long and flat, and from the way things were going, that wasn't changing anytime soon.

"Don't worry, we'll fix that," Lizzie said. She bent into her bag, pulled out a super-frilly tank top and waved it in front of my face.

"What's this?" I snatched it out of her hands and shoved

it back into her bag. I glanced around the hallway to assess the damage. Everyone was walking past and acting like they normally would, so I relaxed a little, glad no one saw the next step in Lizzie's plan. It felt more like Lizzie was making it her personal mission to make a fool out of me.

"Relax, Grace. It's fine. This will be just enough to get the boys to notice."

"Notice what?" Beck asked, joining our group.

"Nothing," I said quickly.

"Did you bring them?" Lizzie asked Beck.

Beck nodded and dug around in his bag until he pulled out a pair of black heels. Lizzie grabbed them eagerly and held them up in the air as if she had won the championship game and was showing off the trophy, except these weren't a prize I wanted. The sky-high heels resembled daggers. I could take someone's eye out with those shoes.

I backed away from her. "No way am I putting shoes like that on."

"Relax, they're perfect. I remembered when Beck's mom wore these to one of our shows. This is the type of shoe that gets people's attention." Lizzie grabbed my hand. "Come on, Grace, let's get you ready before the bell rings. We don't have a lot of time. We'll see you later, Beck. We have girl stuff to do."

She grabbed my arm and yanked me away. I reached my hand out to Beck, hoping he'd grab on and save me, but he only stood there with a perplexed look on his face. "Females," he said. "You're a crazy, crazy bunch."

Lizzie walked past the main bathroom by our lockers and took me through the side hallway to the gym. She pushed open the door and checked under the stalls for feet.

"No one ever uses this bathroom, so we won't be bothered as I work to turn you into a knockout."

She opened her bag and dumped the contents onto the floor. A pile of clothes, makeup, and socks fell out. She picked up a frilly black skirt with poufy stuff under it.

I held it up between two fingers as if it were a dead animal and wrinkled my nose. "What are you turning me into? A clown?"

She pulled it out of my hand and sighed loudly. "Relax, let me do everything and you can complain all you want after. I took these from Amy's room. They worked for her, so they'll have to work for you." She held a sparkly top against me. "Besides, when you see how fabulous you look, you won't want to change back into your boring clothes."

"I'm not wearing any of this," I told her.

"You have to," Lizzie pleaded. "It's part of the plan."

"The plan was to get me noticed, not change me completely. Those things would be ridiculous on me. Especially these awful shoes." I kicked the heels away as if they were on fire.

Lizzie heaved a big sigh but picked up the shoes and put them by her bag. "Maybe a different top?" She started rummaging around in the pile of clothes.

"I'm not changing my clothes," I said to her, and crossed my hands in front of me to let Lizzie know I was willing to stand there all day if that's what it took to get her to lay off her crazy ideas.

"Fine, but can you at least put the tank on? No one will see it under your top, and it will change you enough that the boys will notice something is different but not know what."

"If you can't tell, what's the purpose of putting it on?"

"Just try it, please."

I reluctantly surrendered myself to Lizzie. I grabbed the tank and went into one of the stalls. I had never worn a top like this. Mom bought me two last year, but they were more like cotton tank tops. This one had a little pink bow in the middle and much thinner straps.

I pulled my shirt back on and was walking out to prove to her that it didn't make a difference when the door to the bathroom swung open and in walked none other than Michelle and one of her evil sidekicks, Katie. Of course they would show up to witness this.

I crossed my hands over my chest.

"Hey, Lizard Breath. How cute, the two of you are playing dress-up. That's hisssssterical. Did you get a matching outfit for your dolly?" Michelle asked while Katie made hissing sounds, and I fought the urge to run out of the bathroom and never look back.

"No, you already bought them all out at the store," Lizzie snapped.

"So what's the reason for this little makeover?" Michelle asked. She walked over to the clothes that were still lying on the floor and picked up a black top with a fun rhinestone design on the front. "Wait, never mind, I can see that this is a much-needed improvement over the regular rags that you wear."

I snatched the top out of Michelle's hand, and Lizzie followed my cue. The two of us collected all the other items on the floor and stuffed them into Lizzie's bag. "We're just finishing," Lizzie said. "We'd let you borrow some of these clothes, but I don't think anything could help you."

I followed Lizzie without saying a word. Michelle could dish the insults out, but Lizzie was equally good at dishing them back. Usually that was Beck's job, but I guess when he's not around, Lizzie is his understudy. It felt good to know my friends had my back.

"Don't try to fool yourself, Grace," Michelle said as I was leaving. "You can put on any outfit you want, but just because James is all about kissing you in the show doesn't mean he'll want to keep doing it in real life."

Lizzie yanked me out before I could say anything back, but it didn't matter. In a daze I let her pull me down the hallway. All I could think about was what Michelle had said. James was into kissing me. Me! Lizard breath or not, those were her exact words. Words that simultaneously made me want to break out into song and dance and run back into the bathroom so I could puke in the toilet out of fear.

CHAPTER
Twenty-Seven

LIZZIE LET ME LIVE IN LA-LA LAND OVER what Michelle had said about James for a grand total of ten seconds. After that, she was all business again.

"Listen, we left before I could give you the secret weapon." She ducked into a corner of the hallway where there weren't any lockers and motioned to me to stand close to her.

I felt the straps of the tank digging into my shoulders. "I already have your secret weapon on."

"Here, put these in your top. I'll cover you so no one can see." She pressed two tightly wound balls of socks into my hand as if it was perfectly normal to be forcing your friend to stuff something under her top in the middle of the hallway.

"No way. I may let you talk me into some crazy things, but I have my limits."

"Stop being dramatic. You told me you'd go ahead with the plan. I know for a fact Amy's had about a million boyfriends, so we need to learn from her actions."

"I don't care if she's dated every boy in the world, this is ridiculous."

"Just do it, Grace. You need to trust me."

They were the tiny half socks with the pom-poms on the end. Lizzie had wound them together so they were tight and the pink fuzzy balls were tucked inside. The tank top was one thing, but Lizzie wanted me to stuff it full of something that should be on my feet. I would have laughed at the ridiculousness of it if it wasn't happening to me.

"This isn't the time to be messing around," she said. "Michelle confirmed that James is interested in kissing you."

It was James's name that convinced me. Lizard breath, socks, and fears were pushed aside. I needed to do this. If it helped me get my first kiss before I kissed James, it would be worth it. I hid behind Lizzie and tried my best to shove the socks in where they were supposed to go. Lizzie stepped back and studied me as if she were an artist admiring a painting she created. Too bad I felt like a finger painting instead of a great work of art.

CHAPTER
Twenty-Eight

I WALKED FROM CLASS TO CLASS WITH my hands folded over my chest. I'm sure it made me appear mad and standoffish instead of cute and kissable, but I didn't care. Lizzie, on the other hand, did. She was waiting for a full report when I got to math class.

"Well?" she asked as soon as I sat down. "How is it going with the boys?"

"It's not," I said. "Nothing changed. They keep walking past me as if I don't exist."

"Maybe we should have used more socks," Lizzie mused.

"No way," I practically shouted, and then lowered my

voice when a few kids around us glanced over. "We're not putting any more socks in there."

Mrs. Gutman started class, and I focused on my work, because I didn't want to get called on. We were working through problems on the board, and instead of taking volunteers, she was making people go up. I kept my head down and pretended to be working when she asked for volunteers. My new "chest" jutted out, and I silently cursed Lizzie for talking me into doing something as outrageous as this.

Of course, luck wasn't on my side and it didn't take long before she zeroed in on me to work through the next equation. I looked at the problem on the board, which contained an obscene amount of numbers and decimal points. It was as if she'd saved the worst one for me. I groaned and Lizzie stuck her hand up in the air.

"I know this one, Mrs. Gutman, can I go up and answer it?"

I was so relieved that if we had been any closer, I would have reached out and hugged her. This was the ultimate sacrifice for Lizzie: she was awful at math. And when I say awful, I mean she had a hard time with even simple addition. Once we made cookies and doubled the recipe. Lizzie was the one measuring everything while I mixed, and she messed her math up so bad, the cookies turned into hard, salty rocks. She claimed it was a bad recipe, but no one was buying that. It was her great-grandma's cookie recipe, which had been in the family for generations and never once turned out right when Lizzie made them.

"I think Grace can handle it; we'll let you do the next problem if you're so eager," Mrs. Gutman said.

Lizzie flopped back into her seat and I ran up to the board, happy to have my back facing the class so they couldn't see what kind of enhancements Lizzie had made to my front. I worked my way through the problem and hoped my class couldn't see the lines the tank made against the back of my shirt when I lifted my arm. I had figured out the first two rows of numbers, when I felt something shift under my shirt. I froze and turned my head to look at Mrs. Gutman.

"Are you stuck?" she asked, and it probably made her feel good, since Lizzie and I never stopped talking. I bet she thought it served me right for not paying attention to her lessons.

"No—well, yeah, maybe someone else can give it a try," I said, and started to sweat. This was bad. Very bad.

"I'll walk you through it," she said. "The one you carried was what threw you off. You need to carry two." She pointed to the top of the problem and my heart dropped. Of course it was the number highest up on the board.

"Okay, right, that makes sense," I said, and erased what I had put below the problem when I carried the one. I began to change it, when she spoke up again.

"You want to change that one to a two up top, or you're going to mess yourself up again."

I made eye contact with Lizzie and gestured with my chin down to my chest. Her eyes got wide when she realized what was happening. I reached up slowly to change the number, but it wasn't slow enough. One of the socks slipped out and fell onto the floor. I put my foot over it and hoped against hope that everyone's attention had been on what I was doing on the board and not what happened down below.

No such luck.

"Something fell out of Grace's shirt," a boy named Garrett Huber said, and I wanted to run over and strangle him. Instead, I sent him secret death vibes to be quiet or else. It didn't work. He pointed at the floor. "It's down by her feet."

Mrs. Gutman walked over and picked up the sock. She gave me a puzzled look and then I swear she figured out what it was from. The two of us stood there like deer stuck in headlights. The rest of the class was unusually quiet, waiting to see what would happen.

My mind raced through some of the worst things that had ever happened to me: the time I got my fingers slammed in the car door, or when I was stuck in a bathroom stall without toilet paper. I thought about the time I sneezed in front of Lizzie and Beck and farted by accident. I gathered all these bad things together and guess what? None even came close to what had just happened in front of the entire class. Because none of those situations involved stuffing your tank top with socks and having one fall out onto the floor. None of them!

"Why do you have Grace's dirty sock in your hand?" Garrett shouted to the class, and I wished him a slow, painful death. Why couldn't he shut up?

I needed a plan, and I needed it fast. *Think, think, think,* I told my mind as the seconds ticked by. I was sure everyone in the class was beginning to figure out what really happened. I could practically see the lightbulbs going off over their heads one by one.

Suddenly a solution came to me, and I reached down to smooth my skirt. "Ugh, this dang static. It's been bugging me all day. It was probably stuck to my tights."

"Oh, I hate when that happens," Mrs. Gutman said quickly, catching on and handing the sock back to me.

"My mom is always complaining about how many socks we lose because of static," I said, and hoped the class would buy it. I made a fist over the sock ball and crossed my hands across my now lopsided chest. I rushed back to my seat. Someone else could figure out how to finish the problem on the board—I was dealing with enough problems of my own.

CHAPTER
Twenty-Nine

I AGREED TO GO TO TRICIA'S PARTY ONLY because there wouldn't be anyone from our school there—and on the condition that I was the one who picked out my outfit. Instead of wearing heels and rolled-up socks under my shirt, I opted for jeans and a black sweater with a dark purple T-shirt underneath. I slipped my lucky marble into my back pocket in case it worked on kisses, not just auditions.

"You smell nice," Mom said as she drove me to Lizzie's house, and my palms began to sweat. She was onto me. Had I blown my cover with something as stupid as rose-scented perfume?

"I used some of the perfume Grandma sent me," I told her, which was the truth. What she didn't know was that

I'd sprayed it behind my ears and on my collarbone, places Lizzie's magazine told us were sure to drive a boy wild.

"I guess I'd rather have you go over there looking nice than dressed like a slob. Although I don't think you need to wear perfume to hang out with Lizzie."

"I don't want to hurt Grandma's feelings. She sent it to me as a gift, and I feel bad that I never wear it," I told Mom, but what I really felt awful about was lying to Mom. When we pulled into Lizzie's driveway, I casually glanced next door at Tricia's yard. It looked the same as it always did. I had worried there would be signs of a party, that Mom would suspect things and I'd break down and tell her the truth, and she wouldn't let me go if she found out boys were going to be there. But I didn't have to worry about Mom getting suspicious. A man walked his golden retriever down the block and most of the houses had their front lights on. Nothing seemed out of the ordinary, and it stayed that way as Mom drove away with the promise to come and get me in four hours.

Lizzie didn't even wait for me to ring the doorbell; she threw open the door and came out.

"Let's get moving. We have a party to get to." She slung an arm over my shoulder and pulled me across the lawn. I took in Lizzie's outfit. I might be dressed like plain old Grace, but she had obviously raided her sister's closet. She wore a black sweater dress with gray tights and tall boots. It was a bit rocker chic, except for the red ribbon she tied in her ponytail. "Are you sure you don't want to stay at your place and watch a movie?" I asked her, a last-ditch effort to avoid the party.

"Are you sure you want James to kiss you for the first time in front of a bunch of people?" she shot back.

I gave up and followed her next door. Tricia's parents sat at the kitchen table with another couple. Her mom waved us down toward the basement, but I hung back so Lizzie could go first. I didn't know a soul down there and didn't want to be the first person to walk into the room.

"The party has arrived," Lizzie announced, not caring that she was in a room full of strangers. The girl was brave. A bunch of people looked up to see exactly who was the party, and she waved at them as if she was Miss America walking down the runway.

"See anyone you want to kiss?" she whispered in my ear, and I swatted her away like she was an annoying fly buzzing around me.

"Geez, we just got here. Give me some time to breathe," I told her, but truth be told, I was scanning the room. There were a lot of people squeezed into Tricia's basement, and while most of the boys and girls stayed on opposite sides of the room, it wasn't much different than any other party I'd ever been to. Music played from speakers and someone had taped a HAPPY BIRTHDAY banner and a few bright yellow balloons onto the wall between crepe-paper streamers.

"Hey, girls," Tricia said, coming over to us immediately. "I'm glad you could come."

"Thanks for inviting us," Lizzie said, and smoothed down her dress even though it looked perfect.

"Make sure you check out the cake my mom got me. It's half chocolate and half vanilla." She pointed to the food table that had the cake, bottles of soda lined up next to ice, and bowls of chips. "Help yourself and have fun."

She moved on to another group and Lizzie and I were left alone again.

"Look at all these kissable boys," Lizzie whispered in a voice that was a bit too loud.

I scowled and went over to the snack table before she told the whole room about my lack of kissing experience. I poured a cup of grape soda but avoided the ice, because knowing Lizzie and her crazy scheming, she'd probably try to get me to pretend to choke on an ice cube so we could get one of the boys to perform CPR on me.

"Let's take a seat over there," Lizzie said after she had grabbed a piece of cake. She pointed to a couch where a few boys were sitting.

"Um, no thanks. I'm not going to be the only girl to plant herself in the middle of a group of guys."

"How are you going to get kissed if you don't go where the boys are?" Lizzie asked.

I stared at her in amazement. I didn't know who this girl was. Tonight she had way more guts than I'd ever seen before. Usually Lizzie was as shy as I was around guys, but here she was acting more like her sister. Maybe it was because she wasn't the one hunting for a kiss, so she wouldn't be making a fool out of herself. When someone else was involved, she had nothing to lose.

I glanced around at the boys to see if there was anyone I even would consider kissing but realized there probably wasn't when I saw a group of three boys with pretzels hanging out of their mouths like fangs, chasing some girls.

"I really don't think I'm finding anyone to kiss here," I told Lizzie.

Lizzie put her two hands on my shoulders and leaned so close to me that we were standing nose to nose. I could smell the sour-cream-and-onion chips on her breath. "Grace, this is why we came. This is what you've been searching for. A boy-girl party is the perfect opportunity for a first kiss." She took a step back from me and checked out the room. "I wouldn't mind kissing one of these boys. Guys from Lakewood Academy are so much better-looking than our own."

"I have to disagree," I said as I watched a boy near me chug his soda and let out a huge burp.

She ignored me and pointed to a corner of the room. "Don't you know him? Isn't that your neighbor?"

I followed her gaze and sure enough, Evan was sitting with two other boys, playing some kind of card game. He wore jeans and a long-sleeve T-shirt instead of his standard uniform, but the hat with a professional hockey team on it was a dead giveaway. He hadn't seen me yet, and I felt all nervous for some reason.

"Yeah, that's him," I said softly.

"Let's go talk to him. His friends are cute." She straightened the bow in her hair and tugged at her dress.

"I don't think that's a good idea," I said, because I didn't know how he would act. Lizzie and I were the ones who didn't fit in at this party. This was his school, his friends, and I didn't want to barge in on his conversation. "We can talk to him later when he's not playing cards."

Lizzie seemed content with that promise, and the two of us walked over to a group of girls who were teaching themselves some kind of dance they kept replaying on a laptop. We kicked off our shoes and tried to follow along.

After dancing for a while, I sat in a chair and tried to sneakily watch Evan from the corner of my eye. We should have said something when we got here, because now it was awkward. If I finally did talk to him, what was I going to say? *Hi, Evan, I saw you here an hour ago, but I ignored you because I'm a big wimp.* I put my head in my hands and tried to block out those thoughts.

Maybe that's why I didn't hear my name. Lizzie nudged me in the side. "Um, hello, Grace. There's someone here to talk to you."

I lifted my head and, sure enough, there stood Evan.

"Hey," he said.

"Hi," I said back, not the world's most fascinating conversation.

We didn't get any further than that, because Tricia came over to the three of us.

"Things are kind of boring, don't you think? We need to figure out a way to mix things up so we're all hanging out together."

"Good idea," Lizzie said.

"My family has the game Twister, which might be fun to play, but it's in the storage room. I'd go get it, but I need to keep an eye on things out here."

"Grace can go get it," Lizzie said. "And, Evan, why don't you help her?"

I could see the wheels turning in her head, and I knew exactly what she was planning.

"I don't really know my way around—" I started, but Tricia interrupted.

"All you have to do is go through that door and it's on one of the shelves in the back room."

"Sounds easy enough," Evan said. "Want to go get it, Grace?"

"Yeah, sure," I told him, and stood up.

"This is the perfect chance for a kiss," Lizzie whispered, and slipped a piece of gum into my hand. "Stuff this in your mouth; you're going to be glad you have it."

I stood frozen for a moment, unsure of what to do. How did Evan suddenly go from a friend to someone Lizzie thought I should kiss? She gave me a little push, and I let the gum fall to the ground and slowly followed Evan out of the room. The idea of going to get the game Twister now seemed terrifying.

CHAPTER
Thirty

I WALKED DEEPER INTO THE ROOM AND the sounds of the party got quieter. It smelled like my grand-ma's house, musty and old, and I hoped my perfume was still working. Thankfully, the room wasn't completely dark—there was a small light hanging from the ceiling.

We headed over to the shelves that Tricia was talking about. But what she failed to mention was that there were at least ten of them, stuffed full of junk from floor to ceiling.

"This might take all night," I told him.

"No wonder she didn't want to come back here herself," Evan said, and laughed.

"How about we start in the middle and then move

out from there. That way we don't have to worry about missing it."

"Sounds like a plan," Evan agreed.

The two of us set to work searching through what felt like endless piles and piles of stuff.

After a few minutes, Evan spoke up. "I wasn't expecting you to be here."

"My friend Lizzie talked me into it. She lives next door to Tricia."

"Yeah, I go to school with everyone, so, you know . . ." He trailed off and shrugged. "How's Darby doing? Chase after any more deer lately?"

"No, he's been pretty calm, but I've been keeping a tight hold on his leash."

"You need my protection. Last time it was deer, but you never know when those werewolves might strike."

My stomach did somersaults. Had Evan just told me not to go walking anymore without him? Did that mean he wanted to spend more time with me? Did I want to spend more time with him?

"So . . . um . . . do you think we're going to find this game?" Evan asked, and he moved close enough to me that his arm brushed against mine.

"Tricia acted like her life was going to end if we didn't," I said.

"I'm glad you ended up looking for it with me," Evan said, staring at shelves instead of me.

"You are?" I asked.

"Yeah, I really wanted to tell you—" Evan started, but then he was interrupted by the sound of footsteps.

"Grace Caitlyn Shaw!" a voice yelled. A voice that could only belong to one person.

Mom.

She stood in the open doorway, her hands on her hips. She was at the party, a party I didn't tell her was boy-girl, and she'd found me in the back room alone with Evan.

My life was 100 percent over.

CHAPTER
Thirty-One

"GET OUT," MOM SAID LOUD AND CLEAR so everyone in the room could hear, not that she needed to shout it; it was dead quiet. Someone had turned off the music to ensure the whole world could hear every single word of her tirade, and knowing Mom, she wouldn't disappoint.

I stepped out of the back room without looking at Evan, who I was sure hated me now. Who wouldn't, after her parent busted you in front of everyone?

I didn't dare say anything; I didn't want to give Mom any more ammunition than she needed. She pointed to the steps. "You can head up to the car. Now."

Lizzie was over in one of the corners, hiding behind a

group of kids. Her face had lost its color, and she was crouched down. My guess was she was hoping Mom wouldn't notice her. No such luck; Mom zeroed in on her as quickly as I had.

"Lizzie, your mom wants you home also."

Someone snickered somewhere, and the word "Mommy" was said in a quiet voice. I was dying inside. I moved as quickly as I could to the stairs, but Evan's voice made me stop.

"Mrs. Shaw, we weren't doing anything," he said, and shifted from foot to foot. I could tell he was nervous. "We were looking for a game," he tried to explain, as if he could convince Mom otherwise. He had no clue how to deal with her. She wasn't about to believe him over what she saw.

"Why wasn't Tricia looking for the game? It's her house, isn't it?" she asked, and pursed her lips so they were a thin line across her face. "And do you usually stand that close to someone when you're looking for a game?"

"No, ma'am, you're right," Evan said, and if it was any other situation, I would've laughed at the fact that he was calling Mom a "ma'am."

"I'm not happy about what happened here," she told Evan, and I thought I was going to melt right there into a big puddle of embarrassment.

She made sure Lizzie followed us, and left the room in a

huff of anger and outrage. I walked behind her with no complaint, because I wanted out of there. Whatever Mom had to say, it needed to be done outside, away from everyone. I got into the car without even saying good-bye to Lizzie. Mom followed and slammed her door shut.

She drove for a while, not saying a word, and there was no way I was going to be the one to start the conversation. Instead, I tried to think of happy thoughts, like Evan telling me he was glad we went to look for the game together and wondering what it was he'd tried to tell me. Things to take my mind off the smackdown Mom was no doubt about to lay on me.

It wasn't until we pulled into Cravings, our favorite coffee shop, that I knew what she was waiting for. This was going to be a serious talk.

While Lake Erie was my special place to go with Dad, Cravings was the place Mom and I went to for girl talks. We usually ended up there when Claire was at a friend's house or soccer practice. The place was full of big, comfy chairs that made me feel tiny when I sat in them. I always got hot chocolate and put tons of whipped cream on top. Somehow that helped make any talk better, but tonight even a couple of cans of whipped cream wouldn't make this conversation easy.

"Go ahead and pick out some seats," Mom said after we both got our drinks.

I staked my claim to the chairs in a back corner, far away from the big tables full of people who were talking and laughing, as Mom grabbed napkins and stirrers. I played with the whipped cream on the top so I wouldn't have to make eye contact with her.

"So," Mom said. "Did you really think it was okay to lie about where you were going to be and go to a party without asking me first?"

"We were only next door at Tricia's house. Lizzie and I have gone over there before and you've never seemed to mind." I sunk deep into the leather chair and hoped no one could hear what we were talking about.

"The difference is, those others times it was you, Lizzie, and Tricia. Not the three of you and a room full of boys."

"There were girls, too," I said, trying to make it sound better, but Mom's eyes flashed with anger.

"Don't get smart with me," she said, and I knew I needed to come clean with Mom if I wanted to get out of this place alive.

"I meant that it was a party full of people."

"You weren't at that part of the party when I showed up.

You were alone with a boy," Mom said, and even I had to admit that this sounded bad.

"We were looking for a game," I said. "Tricia wanted to play Twister, so we went back to find it. Evan and I weren't doing anything but talking. We talk sometimes in the morning when I'm waiting for the bus. I swear that's all that happened. I didn't kiss him, if that's what you're worried about. We're just friends. We can go over and knock on his door if you want me to prove it." I *didn't* want to prove it, but anything was better than having Mom mad at me. Scratch that—anything was better than having disappointed Mom, because that's what I felt like I had done. That wasn't the type of person I was, but now, with Operation Pucker Up, it seemed as if I was someone else.

"I don't think that's necessary," she said.

"Tonight was a mistake, and you don't need to worry about me. I've never kissed anybody, and that's not going to change anytime soon." I blew on my hot chocolate and watched the steam rise up from it.

"Oh, honey," she said, and placed her hand on mine. It was warm and felt good. Comforting. "You don't need to kiss someone. You're young. Enjoy being a kid. Believe me, kissing complicates things."

"You've got that right," I agreed. I didn't mention the play; I couldn't. It was the last thing I wanted to think about. Besides, that was a fake kiss. A kiss that someone was making us do. What I was talking about with Mom was a real kiss, and that was never going to happen.

Mom picked up her coffee and took a big sip of it. She looked me straight in the eye as she put it down. "I didn't have my first kiss until I was a sophomore in high school. I felt like there was something wrong with me, but once I got that kiss, it was all worth the wait. Maybe your perfect kiss isn't here yet."

"You didn't kiss anyone until high school?"

"Nope, and I worried about it all the time. But in the end, I'm glad I waited."

I thought about the stories Mom and Dad used to tell. The ones about how they were high school sweethearts, and it didn't take me long to put two and two together. "Dad was your first kiss?"

"Yep, and the whole thing was pretty awkward." There was a funny, faraway expression on her face, and the left side of her mouth kept turning up in a little smile. I could practically see her reliving that first kiss, which was so gross. I must have made a face, because Mom's face turned serious again.

"You need to be easier on your father, Grace. He loves you. He loves all of us, and we need to work together to become a family again."

"You, me, and Claire were doing fine without him," I argued.

"We're a family of four, honey. We need to be together."

"How can you be on his side?" I asked. "He left us." I felt tears coming, and I fought hard to keep them back.

Mom played with her napkin, tearing pieces off of it. "He didn't leave you. It's hard for you to understand now, but we needed that break."

"How can you say he didn't leave us?" I couldn't believe Mom was sticking up for Dad. Not after how sad he made her. "He walked away from our house and our lives. He didn't even come to my play. He came to every play I've ever been in, and then he didn't. I waited for him every single night. I tried to find him in the audience, and when I couldn't find him, I still hoped that he would show up backstage after the show. But he didn't. He wasn't there and he wasn't in our lives. Don't say he didn't leave us."

I wadded up one of the napkins on the table and tossed it on the floor in anger. I glared at Mom, daring her to tell me I was wrong.

Mom closed her eyes and took a deep breath. "That was my fault. His leaving was still too new, too fresh. I asked him not to come to the play, because I knew if I saw him, I'd let him come back home to us. Just like I asked him to give us space all those months. I needed time. We needed time. He listened to me because he was willing to do whatever he needed to in order to fix things."

"You caused him to miss my show? Why didn't you tell me the truth? All this time, I thought it was because of me. That he didn't want to see me." My voice rose as the realization of what Mom had said sank in, and I fought to keep it down, so I wouldn't make a scene. I'd be lying if I said I wasn't upset at Mom for keeping this from me.

Mom sighed and ran her hands through her hair. She looked tired and sad.

"I was there every night, helping with the show. I couldn't back out of the commitment, but I also couldn't see him there."

"Why couldn't he have come in a different door? Walked in when the lights went down? You could have figured it out."

"I wasn't thinking straight then. I can't ask you to understand, but please don't blame your dad. If you want to blame anyone, blame me."

I swirled what was left of my hot chocolate around in my mug. My mind was spinning. I heard what Mom was saying, but nothing made sense.

"I need you to give him a chance," Mom said. "It's hard, but he's a good father. He loves you. He loves us. We need to be a family again. Can you try to do that?"

I nodded, but I wanted to ask what made her so sure that if we let Dad back into our lives now and tried to become a family again, it would work.

"What do you say we head home?" she asked, but I needed to talk to her about one more thing.

"Are you going to tell Dad what happened tonight?" This conversation felt like one big episode of déjà vu, but I couldn't have Mom talking. If she told Dad what happened, he'd tell Mom about the near-kiss in the theater, and I'd be in deep, deep trouble. I was setting the two of them up to basically keep secrets from each other, but I needed to. It was unavoidable, because what else was I supposed to do?

"I need to tell your father," Mom, the rule-follower, said.

"No, you don't." I begged in the way Mom hated when Claire and I did it for something, but I needed to make her understand. "It was embarrassing enough for you to find Evan and me together; I'll die if you tell Dad. You want me to be close to him again, but how can I if I'm too embarrassed to be around him?"

It was sneaky, and I felt guilty about using Mom's words like that, but I was desperate. There was no doubt in my mind that Mom would yank me from the show if she found out about the other incident.

"Your father cares about you. He wants the best for you, just like me," Mom said, but I could tell she was weakening, because she got that faraway look in her eyes that meant she was thinking hard about something. "Do you understand why I'm so upset about what I walked into at that party? Lizzie's mom needed to tell me where you were when I came to her door to pick you up. Not only did you lie to me, but you put yourself in a position with a boy that you knew you shouldn't be in."

"I'm sorry," I said for what I figured was the millionth time that day.

"I want your first kiss to be something special. Don't rush things."

"I won't." I made a decision. If Mom would stay quiet, I would give up Operation Pucker Up. Forget about learning how to kiss so I wouldn't look stupid in front of James. This wasn't about him anymore. I didn't know what it was about, and until I could figure that out, I was done trying to kiss people.

"I won't tell your father, but I think it would be a good idea if you hung around the house for the next two weeks. Spend some time with your family instead of your friends. I want you coming straight home after rehearsals," she said, and I understood that that this was her way of telling me I was grounded. Truthfully, I'd endure whatever she wanted me to do if she didn't tell Dad. "And you need to promise me that you'll think things through more in the future. You're a smart, beautiful girl. You do so much every single day that makes me proud. Don't worry about this stuff yet."

I could hear her voice wavering a little bit at the end, and if we weren't in a crowded coffee shop, I would have hugged her. Instead, I settled on picking up her hand and giving it a squeeze.

CHAPTER
Thirty-Two

MOM WENT TO CHECK ON CLAIRE WHEN we got home, so I went into my room and turned on my walkie-talkie.

"Grace? Are you there?" Lizzie asked when I made it up to my room. She was waiting for me. I should have known she'd also want to talk about everything that happened.

"I'm here," I said. I tried to keep my voice down so Mom wouldn't come and investigate what I was up to. I couldn't imagine what would happen if we lost our walkie-talkies right smack-dab in the middle of one of the worst nights of my life.

"Thank goodness. I was about to go crazy over here."

"Tell me about it," I said. "Tonight was awful." I looked

out my window as I talked to her and tried to figure out who the shadows behind Evan's curtains belonged to.

"More like mortifying. I can't believe your mom yanked us out of the party like that."

"Yeah," I said, playing with the cord on my window blinds. "It wasn't the best way to leave the party."

"Hello, it was the worst," Lizzie said in a voice so loud that I had to turn down the volume on the walkie-talkie. "This was our big night to meet new people, and you hardly talked to anyone. Then your mom showed up and ruined everything. Tricia will probably never talk to me again, forget ever inviting me to a party."

"I'm sorry. I didn't know my mom would show up like that."

There was a pause and then Lizzie demanded, "Well? I think you have some information to share with me."

"I do?" I asked, confused.

"What happened with you and Evan?"

"Nothing happened. Nothing at all," I said. I watched the blob in my lava lamp move slowly up and down. "What made you think it was okay to tell Tricia that the two of us would go find the game together?"

"I was only trying to help."

"Your *help* didn't work."

"Forget him," Lizzie said. "We'll move on to someone bigger and better. I'm not giving up on Operation Pucker Up."

"I'm done chasing after boys," I told her.

"You know, Grace, I'm starting to wonder about you." Lizzie sighed as if she didn't know what to do with me. "It's like you don't care about Operation Pucker Up at all."

Lizzie didn't know how right she was about that, and if I was truthful about OPU, it was probably time to admit to her that I was never really into it.

"From the beginning, you knew it made me uncomfortable, but I went along with it anyway."

"How can you say that? I did this for you because you're my friend."

"It didn't feel right," I told her. "Trying to get a kiss from someone just to kiss them."

"Why didn't you say anything?" Lizzie asked.

"I did. I tried to, but you wouldn't listen. Just like all the times I tried to talk to you about my dad and you ignored me. You were too excited about my part in the play and then about Operation Pucker Up to think about how I might feel."

Lizzie got quiet, and for a minute I thought she had turned off her walkie-talkie, but then she spoke up. "I didn't mean to do that. I was happy for you and wanted to help."

"I know," I told her. I hated fighting with my best friend, but this had gone on for too long. "I just need to you to stop and listen to me when I try to talk to you. And I promise to listen to your ideas too, because some of them are good. I know you were only trying to help me with OPU."

"Maybe we can talk at lunch Monday. About your dad," Lizzie said.

"I'd like that a lot," I said.

"Then you're not mad?"

"Nope. Are you mad at me?"

"How could I be mad at my best friend?" Lizzie said, and I couldn't agree more.

"Best friends forever," I told her.

"And ever," she said.

The two of us said good night, and it felt like all was okay between Lizzie and me again.

I buried myself under my covers, glad to have my best friend understand me and ready to put this night behind me. All I wanted was for things to go back to the way they were before we started OPU. I was tired of life shaking things up for me over and over again. I was ready to accept the fact that this love stuff wasn't for me.

 181

CHAPTER
Thirty-Three

SINCE I'D MADE THE DECISION TO QUIT Operation Pucker Up, I figured it was time to let Mrs. Hiser know my secret. I needed to buy some extra time for myself, and the best way to do that was to come clean to her and lay it all on the line. She was a woman, and at some point in her life she must have worried about her first kiss too. This was it. I needed to sit down and talk to her, woman to woman.

I stopped by her classroom before the school day started so we would be alone. I ran my finger over my lucky marble, which I seemed to be relying on more and more lately.

She was straightening papers and singing when I walked up.

"Mrs. Hiser?" I asked, and she jumped.

"Oh, sorry, Grace. I was off daydreaming." She laughed, and it helped me relax. I knew exactly what she meant about being in dreamland; I pretty much felt as if I was living there full-time now.

"Can I talk to you for a minute?"

"Sure." She took a seat on her piano bench and gestured toward the metal chair nearby. "What's up?"

"It's the play," I began, and stared at a small stain on the floor in front of me. I rolled my marble around and around in my hand. "I'm so lucky to be playing Snow White, and I love all of it, but there's a problem."

"Let's see if I can fix it. What's the matter?" She asked it in a way that was so nice and caring, but somehow the words were stuck to the roof of my mouth like when I put too much peanut butter on my sandwich and take a huge bite. Why was it so hard to admit the truth to people sometimes?

"Well, everything is okay until the end. . . ."

"And then?" she prompted.

"Then . . ."

"It's okay, Grace. What you say here stays between us," Mrs. Hiser said.

"It's the kiss," I said, the words out there in the open. There was no turning back now.

"Ahh . . . the kiss," Mrs. Hiser repeated. "I have a feeling I know what we're going to be talking about here."

"You do?" I asked, surprised, but then, maybe I shouldn't have been. Mrs. Hiser had been directing plays for years, and she'd probably had to deal with plenty of kisses. Heck, she might have even been through a situation like this already. The thought that maybe I wasn't alone, that maybe someone else had had to face this same thing, gave me the courage to keep talking. "The thing is, I've never kissed anyone before." I paused, took a deep breath, and let it all come out. "And every time I think about having to kiss James, it scares the heck out of me."

"Thanks for speaking up. Sometimes I forget you're all kids playing the parts of grown-ups. I get so swept up in the story and the world you create onstage that I don't stop to think about things like this." Mrs. Hiser smiled, but it wasn't in a way like she was laughing or making fun of me. Instead, she looked as if she genuinely cared about me and my fears. "You have a right to worry about this, Grace. I wouldn't want to have my first kiss in front of a bunch of people either."

 184

"Exactly," I said, so glad that she understood. "That's what I keep thinking about. I try to get excited about the play and then it all goes back to the kiss."

"Well, we can't let Snow White sleep through the end of the play," she said, and I felt my heart drop. Great. She understood, but she wasn't going to do anything to help. I was doomed; it was like this kiss was a curse someone cast on me.

"Yeah, I know," I said, and tried to make it sound as if things were okay when they very much weren't. "I'll figure it out."

"No, no, no," Mrs. Hiser said. "We have options. What if we changed the ending of the play and he didn't kiss you? It wouldn't be the traditional story, but who says we can't mix things up?"

"I don't think that would work," I said, because even if she thought of some other amazing way to wake up Snow White, Michelle and company would never let me live it down. Everyone knows the way *Snow White* was supposed to go. Michelle would jump at the chance to make sure the world knew I was the loser who couldn't kiss Prince Charming in the play.

"We could block the scene in a way that the audience

185

won't be able to tell if James is kissing you. He can do an air kiss, if that's more comfortable for you. What do you think?"

I played with my marble, opening and closing my palm around it, as I thought about what Mrs. Hiser said. An air kiss would be easier. It would solve all my problems, and life would definitely be a lot better if this awful kiss just went away.

"We can practice the scene again at the next rehearsal to make sure it works," she continued.

I froze. I could just picture Michelle and her crew watching James and me do a fake kiss. There's no way they wouldn't call me out on it. Michelle had made it her life's mission to make sure I failed at the role of Snow White. She'd spot our air kiss from a mile away and make sure everyone noticed it. The entire cast would discover what a wimp I was, and I'd never get a good part again.

No way. I couldn't let that happen. I was an actress, after all, and I should be able to play any role that I was cast in. There were people who played cold-blooded murderers in movies, and if they were able to do that, I should certainly be able to handle a kiss.

Mrs. Hiser could sense my hesitation. "How about you think about things? You don't need to decide right now. And in the meantime, we'll practice the scene without the kiss until you figure out what you're the most comfortable with."

"Thanks," I said, and my body relaxed. I was glad that at least I'd bought myself a little bit more time, even if I still didn't have my happily ever after yet.

CHAPTER Thirty-Four

EVAN WAS OUTSIDE WHEN LIZZIE'S MOM dropped me off after rehearsal that day. He was hitting a tennis ball against the garage door with his hockey stick. I listened to it smack the surface a few times before I coughed so he'd notice me. He gave me a little wave, and I couldn't help but give him a big smile back.

Mom continued to make it clear that I was grounded. I wasn't sure if crossing the grass to Evan's yard was allowed, but it was a risk I was willing to take.

"I don't think a goalie can stop any of your shots," I joked, and let my book bag swing down off my shoulder and onto the ground. I crossed over to his yard to watch.

"I know, right? I'm on fire." He put his stick down and wiped some sweat from his forehead. "So how are things with your mom?"

"I've pretty much signed my life away until I'm an old lady, but at least she lets me out for fresh air once in a while," I joked.

"Yeah, my parents weren't too happy that I was alone in the room with you. I wasn't allowed to go to my hockey game the next day and I have to unload the dishwasher for the next two weeks."

"Sorry about that," I told him. "I told my mom not to call your parents, but she wasn't going to listen to me."

"It's okay, my parents would have done the same thing. So . . . are you able to go anywhere right now?" Evan asked.

"I don't know—" I started, but he cut me off.

"Because I want to show you something really cool."

I felt a little shiver of excitement. Evan wanted to spend time with me? I thought about what it might mean and what I should do. Mom had watched me like a hawk since the night of the party and she was making sure I followed her punishment. But this afternoon she wasn't home. She had the day off work, so she was helping to coach Claire's game because another mom was out sick. And Dad wouldn't be home until dinnertime.

"It will be worth it," he said. "Want to go?"

I looked from my house to Evan, back and forth, debating. If I made it back before Mom came home, no one would know.

"Okay, but I can't stay out too long."

"I'll make sure to get you back in time," he said, and gestured to me to follow him.

The two of us walked next to each other on the sidewalk for a while, not saying anything. I followed him until he stopped and pointed to an old, worn-out dirt path that cut behind some houses. Tree branches hung low and weeds threatened to take over, as if staking claim. It seemed very much like this was a place we shouldn't be walking. Evan started down, and I shrugged. I had already broken one rule by leaving the house—why not break another one?

Evan stopped once we reached the train tracks. This is where he wanted to take me? Or from the look of things, our destination was the steps that led up to a rusted metal bridge that went over the tracks. Evan began to climb them.

I may have been okay with following him down the path, but there was no way in the world that he was going to get me on those steps, especially since there was a big sign over them that said NO TRESPASSING.

"You have to be kidding," I told him.

"The sign is there to cover the city's butt. They closed off the steps years ago when people were tossing rocks down at the trains. We're not planning on doing that, are we?"

"I hope not."

"Let's go. It's perfectly safe on the bridge," he said, and as if to prove it to me, he ducked under the sign and climbed up the steps. He waved at me to do the same, but I shook my head. He would have to come back down and drag me up there if he wanted me on the steps.

"What do I have to do?" Evan yelled. "Come down and carry you up?"

I busted out laughing, which relaxed me a little bit. "Are you a mind reader?"

"Yep, and now I can see that in your mind, you want to join me."

"Fine," I said. Even if it scared the heck out of me, I did want to be up there. "But if this bridge collapses and the police show up to arrest us, I'm blaming it on you."

Evan held up his hands. "I take all responsibility. Now hurry up."

My first steps were tentative, but after I made it up a few

steps and nothing horrible happened, I continued a bit faster, trusting that everything would be okay.

Once I reached the top, I stared across to the other side, where another set of steps was. You could stand right over the tracks, which was exactly what Evan was doing and exactly what I didn't want to do. The sides of the bridge were high, so I would have to stand on my tiptoes to see over.

"Come out to the middle," Evan called. "We don't have much time."

"Time until what?" I asked. I tried to step out onto the bridge. The bottom was a grid; the ground showed through the holes. I moved right back. I might be able to climb up the stairs, but walking out across the tracks when I could see straight down was a whole different story. "I don't think I can do this."

"Grab on, I'll help you." Evan held out his hand. I wrapped my fingers around his and took tiny steps toward him. I focused on the warmth of his hand and not on the ground that was far below me. I tried not to think about how terrifying it was.

"I told you it was easy," he said, and squeezed my hand. I glanced at our two hands together. I willed Evan not to let go, but he did as he fished out his cell phone from his pocket and checked it. "Now all we have to do is listen. It should be here any minute."

"What should?"

"The five p.m. coal train." Evan said it as if it was no big deal that a giant train was going to go roaring past under us. "It stops my dad at the railroad crossing every day on his way home from work; he's always complaining about it."

"I don't think I can do this," I said, but Evan nodded his head slowly.

"Trust me, you can. You don't want to miss it. You can shout it all out."

"Shout it out?" What the heck was he talking about?

"All the things that are making you upset. Go ahead and name something."

"What upsets you?" I asked, not exactly comfortable at the idea of spilling my guts to Evan.

"A lot of things, but mostly my grandma and her sickness." Evan said. "What about you?"

I definitely couldn't tell him about Operation Pucker Up. But . . . "My dad," I said, even though my mind told me to be quiet and not tell Evan about my problems. But another part of me told me it was time to stop holding all these feelings in.

It seemed like Evan got me and understood what it felt like to have your life turned upside down.

"Talk about it. You need to say this stuff out loud for this to work." Evan stood right in front of me. I met his gaze and made the decision to tell him the truth. No more hiding stuff because I was afraid of what people might think. I wanted to tell someone what I thought.

"I'm mad at him for coming back into my house."

"And?"

"For acting as if he was allowed to be a part of our lives again."

A horn blew in the distance and Evan jumped up, grabbing my hand for the second time that day.

"This is it," he said. "Keep talking. Let it out. It's the only way."

The train was getting closer. Not only could I hear the horn, but I could feel the rumbling of the wheels. The bridge shook and Evan squeezed my hand even harder.

"I'm mad that my grandma is sick," he shouted. "It's not fair. My grandma is a good person. She shouldn't be going through this. We shouldn't."

He yelled with such intensity that it finally made sense to me. I could see his shoulders relaxing and his grip on my hand loosened, as if speaking those words out loud helped him.

"I'm mad at my dad," I said, testing out the words against the rising sound of the train.

"Tell it to the air," he said.

And I did. I opened my mouth and tried to yell over the train that was getting closer and closer. A tiny speck of light appeared in the distance and the bridge beneath me vibrated. I watched the light grow bigger and bigger as the train barreled toward us. The conductor laid on the horn again, and I could barely hear Evan yelling into the air.

"It's not right. This should be my time. Mine. I finally got a lead in the play, a big part, but no one cares. No one!" I yelled.

The bridge was now shaking so hard that it felt as if it could collapse, but it didn't, and with Evan's hand in mine, it felt like the safest place in the world now that I was telling the truth.

"All anyone thinks about is becoming a family again," I shouted, and my voice broke, straining as I tried to be heard over the thundering of the train. "As if we can just pick up the pieces. No one remembers what Dad did to us. I'm mad at all of them. Not only Dad, but Mom and my sister, for letting him come back."

The train rolled under us, and it was as if I became encased in a bubble of noise, movement, and vibration. Below my feet, it seemed as if the top of the train almost skimmed the bridge we were on. The cars changed as each rolled past, some with black metal tops, others open and full of black coal. A hot wind from the train's speed blew my hair around as we screamed out our fears, letting the power of it move through our bodies. And the entire time, Evan held tight to my hand, and I held on to him.

It took a few minutes for the train to pass, and I yelled until my voice was hoarse and my throat burned.

I turned and watched the end of the train as it disappeared, retreating into the distance. Dust and leaves danced around us, the world stirred up and disturbed.

"No one cares," I whispered, and realized my face was wet with tears.

"I care," Evan said.

I thought about what he had done for me. Evan understood what everyone else ignored, and that made all the difference. At least for a moment, I wasn't alone.

"Thanks," I said.

He dropped his hand from mine, ran it through his hair, and shifted from foot to foot. "It's my favorite spot to go to when I need to shout at the world. Because once the train comes, no matter how loud I yell, I can't hear its response."

"Sometimes that's exactly the way it needs to be," I said, and it was true. Evan had given me what I couldn't find for myself: the courage to speak up about what was bothering me instead of holding my problems inside.

CHAPTER
Thirty-Five

THE WALK BACK TO MY HOUSE SEEMED a lot faster than the walk to the bridge, and when we got to Evan's front yard, I didn't want to go inside. Mom's car was in the driveway, so whatever waited inside for me wasn't going to be good. The two of us leaned up against the back of Evan's mom's minivan, using it to shield us from both our houses.

"Thanks again," I said, playing with an imaginary piece of lint on my shirt.

"No problem," Evan answered, acting as weird as me. He pulled on the two strings that hung from his hooded sweatshirt.

"It really helped."

"Maybe I could go to your play," Evan said to the ground, not looking up at me. It came out fast and his words mashed together, but I understood what he was asking me. "I mean, if you don't mind?"

"I don't mind," I said, and didn't bother to hide the smile that threatened to take over my face. But then it hit me.

Evan wanted to come to my play.

The play where I kiss James.

There was no way he could come to opening night. No way, nohow. It was bad enough the world would have to witness our kiss; Evan was not going to watch that.

"I think opening night is sold out, but you could go Saturday," I said.

"Sure, I can go to any of the shows."

"I mean that opening night is always so hectic and people don't have everything right and we're nervous—"

"Relax, Grace. I won't come to opening night. But I don't think you need to worry about being nervous about the kiss—"

Evan stopped and put his hand over his mouth like a little kid who was caught saying something bad.

I froze. Was I hearing things? Did Evan just mention the kiss?

"What are you talking about?" I asked very slowly, afraid to hear his answer.

"I meant how the prince has to kiss Snow White at the end, and . . ."

"No," I said. "That's not what you meant." I tilted my head and squinted at him, as if he were some science experiment I was observing, as if I could figure out what was going on, because this didn't make sense at all. "You said I didn't need to worry about being nervous about the kiss. How did you know I was worried about it?"

"It was stupid of me to say, Grace. It's nothing," he said, but it *was* something.

"Tell me how you knew," I demanded, drawing on my acting skills to make myself sound strong and tough. Truthfully, I wanted to crumble into a ball, because I was terrified of what Evan's slipup might mean.

I could tell he wanted to turn and run away, but I wasn't going to give him that option. I stared him down and tried to look mean and intimidating.

"I heard you and Lizzie talking about it," he said.

"No," I said, shaking my head back and forth.

"I'm really sorry—"

"How?" I asked, cutting him off. What he was saying didn't make sense, and I didn't want to believe that he knew. Where would he have heard Lizzie and me? He didn't go to my school, and ever since Dad came home, I didn't dare let her come over and see the mess that was our family.

"On the walkie-talkies. I picked up some of your conversations. I didn't mean to, but we got a set for my grandma so she could communicate with us when we were upstairs in case she needed something. One night I heard other voices coming through, and when I listened, I realized it was you and Lizzie."

"What did you hear?" I asked. My face grew hot with embarrassment, and I wanted to cry.

Evan shook his head quickly.

"What did you hear?" I repeated, and tried to remember all the things Lizzie and I discussed.

"You two, talking about Operation Pucker Up," Evan said quietly. It sounded so wrong hearing that name come out of his mouth. Operation Pucker Up was private; it was not something Evan should ever know about. I felt my face begin to heat up with embarrassment.

"That was private. How could you listen to us?" I asked, and tried very hard not to cry.

He didn't dare meet my eyes, and it was a good thing he didn't, because I didn't think I could keep back the tears that were threatening to spill out. This was mortifying. I turned around and ran home, wishing Lizzie had never, ever created Operation Pucker Up.

CHAPTER
Thirty-Six

THE HUMILIATION THAT WAS MY LIFE didn't end when I walked into the house. My parents practically tackled me in a fight to see who could yell at me first. I was surprised to see Dad home, but I guess a missing daughter excuses you from doing the weather.

"Where have you been?" Mom demanded.

I closed my eyes and prayed she hadn't seen me out there with Evan. I tried to think of a good excuse and wished I had thought to bring Darby with me.

She didn't give me a chance to come up with an answer; she launched right back into her yelling.

"We've been worried sick for over an hour. And you

weren't even supposed to be leaving this house, after what happened at Tricia's party."

"Tricia's party?" Dad asked, and I knew it was all over. My whole entire life. I saw it flash before my eyes.

"It was nothing," I said, hoping maybe he would be gullible enough to believe it was nothing.

"Wait, wait, wait," Dad said. "Who is Tricia and what happened at her party?"

I caught Mom's eye and shook my head.

Please, please, please stay quiet.

Nope, not a chance. She was too mad at me right now.

"I went to pick Grace up from Lizzie's house the other night and she wasn't there. It turned out she was next door at Tricia's house. In a room alone with a boy."

"It wasn't like that," I interrupted. Why did Mom have to make it sound so awful and bad? "We went to find a game, and we were only talking. We weren't doing anything."

Dad walked back and forth across the room, very quickly. It felt worse that he wasn't saying anything. I knew without a doubt he was thinking about the promise I made not to let something like this happen again.

"Grace, I thought we were clear on everything," Dad finally said. "You told me nothing like this would happen again."

"We weren't doing anything," I repeated again, my voice rising loud and frantic.

"That's the same thing you said to Mr. O'Malley and me. Something tells me I've been played for a fool. By both you and your mother."

"What do you mean, she said it before to Mr. O'Malley?" Mom asked.

This was it.

The end.

"Oh, it's nothing," I said quickly, but I could tell by the way Dad narrowed his eyes at me that he wasn't going to keep my secret anymore.

"I was called in to Grace's school recently. She was caught backstage with Beck by Mr. O'Malley. He found them alone and it looked very much like they had every intention in the world to kiss."

If I could have vanished right then and never come back, I would have. At that moment, there was no way in the world I could imagine any positive outcome for me after this conversation.

"Is this true?" Mom asked me, and I nodded, keeping my eyes on my shoes. They were covered in dirt from hiking through the path to the bridge with Evan.

I waited for Mom to explode, and she did—but it wasn't at me. Instead, she took a deep breath and stood up straight. She wasn't much taller than five feet, but suddenly, in front of Dad, she was a giant.

"Can you please tell me why you thought you didn't need to tell me that you were called into school to speak to the principal because my daughter was found in the theater with a boy?"

"It's not as bad as it sounds," he said. Great, now he'd decided to help me out again. *Too late, Dad.* Mom was in battle mode and there was no way I'd win this one.

"That's not for you to decide," Mom said, her voice getting louder and louder. "She's my daughter; I should have known what was going on. Instead, you decide to keep this from me."

"Oh really?" Dad shot back. "I'm the bad guy? Because I just found out about a party Grace went to where you found her in a room with a boy. Seems as if I'm not the only one keeping secrets around here."

"Don't you dare turn this around on me," Mom said, her voice all high-pitched and loud.

I couldn't take it anymore. I couldn't listen to the two of them go through this again.

"Stop it!" I yelled, so loud that I was surprised the windows didn't rattle. "I'm standing right here. Stop arguing like I'm not in the room."

"You're right, Grace, we shouldn't be doing this here—" Mom started, but I held up my hand. I didn't want to hear any more, and I needed to get this out before I pushed it deep down inside me again.

"You shouldn't be doing it at all. Dad moved back in because you two wanted to be together. You can't act like this. Not again."

I stopped to catch my breath. I was breathing hard, as if I had run a race. My body shook, and I felt as if my legs could give out on me at any moment. I needed to get away from them, but instead of going to my room and slamming my door like I usually would, I took a different tack. I walked up the steps quiet and civilized and acted as if I was indestructible. As if Mom and Dad could do nothing to hurt me. I waited until I was in my room to let myself fall apart.

Is this what love was? Is this why people wanted to be together? Why would someone choose this? If this is what happens when you love someone, then forget it. I don't want to have any part of it.

I turned my walkie-talkie on, hoping that Lizzie and Evan were listening.

"Operation Pucker Up is over," I said after I pressed down on the red button. "I'm done with it."

I repeated this over and over again. I kept my hand on the button to make sure there was no way anyone on the other end could get a word in. This wasn't a conversation, it was my last and final statement.

CHAPTER
Thirty-Seven

MY PARENTS LEFT ME ALONE FOR THE rest of the night. I kept waiting for a knock on my door, but it never came.

They may not have talked to me, but they did talk to each other. I could hear their hushed voices through my wall, like I used to in the past when Dad would come home from another late night at work. Except this time, their voices stayed low and even. I'm not sure what it meant, but I was eventually able to fall asleep instead of staying up afraid of how this fight would end.

I was confused when I woke up the next morning and the house smelled delicious. Something was going on, because my parents never, ever baked. Dad stank at it and Mom claimed there were no circumstances that would inspire her enough to grab a cookbook, get her measuring cup, and switch on the oven. Especially when baking required her to use her arch-enemy, sugar.

"It involves too many specifics," Mom would say. "You have to measure, separate, and follow rules or it doesn't turn out right."

Claire and I would beg Mom for homemade birthday cakes or Christmas cookies, but she'd shake her head, swearing off baking for life. On the few occasions she actually allowed us to have sugar, it came from some store-bought treat. Talk about missing out.

But today was different: all I needed to do was follow the scent to see that Mom had indeed cracked open a recipe book, and I hoped I was on the receiving end of whatever she was making.

I wandered into the kitchen, still in my pajamas, and decided not to say anything about the day before until they did. Instead, I slumped down at the table across from Dad, who paged through the newspaper. I grabbed a random section and pretended I was interested in it, even after I saw that

I was looking at the used-car advertisements and had no use for a car for a few more years.

Mom put a plate of blueberry pancakes in front of Dad and me, which made me question this whole scenario. I wondered if I was dreaming when she added a big container of warm maple syrup to the table.

"Is this for real?" I asked, breaking the silence.

"What?" Mom asked.

"The pancakes. And the syrup. You never let us have something as sugary as syrup first thing in the morning."

"Well, maybe it's time I do," Mom said, and grabbed a plate of her own from near the stove. She sat down with us and picked up the container of syrup. "I need to learn that the world isn't going to end if I bend the rules or drench my pancakes in syrup, which I fully intend to do."

"Sugar is very, very good for you," I told her in between bites.

Dad set his paper to the side and dug into his own pancakes. He shoved bites into his mouth as if they were going to disappear.

"Where's Claire?" I asked. Claire never slept in, and she would be the first one to the table when something that promised to be unhealthy was served.

"I ran her over to the Conways' house. We wanted to talk to you alone."

I set my fork down. Here it was, the big punishment. I put my elbows on the table even though Mom loathed it. *Go for it,* I thought. *I can take it.* Because at this point, nothing could be worse than Evan knowing all my secrets. Well, almost anything.

"Please, please, please don't make me quit the show," I begged. "I'll do anything else you tell me to do; don't take that away."

"We're not going to make you quit the show," Mom said. "And while you're pretty much grounded for life after what you've done these past few weeks, that's not what we want to talk about."

"You don't?" I asked. I let out a deep breath I didn't even realize I was holding. Thank goodness the play was still happening, even if the rest of my life wasn't.

"We haven't been fair to you about the separation. We acted as if you understood why we needed to take a break, and that wasn't right. Our separation wasn't something you should have to understand."

"I'm not so young," I told my parents, mad they were assuming otherwise. "I get what's going on."

"Maybe some of it," Dad said. "But we should have talked to you more. Explained things."

"I . . . we . . . haven't been honest with you," Mom said. She took a sip of coffee before she spoke again. "And now I realize how unfair that has been to you."

Dad put his elbows on the table too, and leaned toward me, the pancakes forgotten by all of us. "There are things that went on between us that are private, things we'll always keep private, but where we went wrong is not talking enough to you."

"Dad and I didn't talk to each other," Mom said. "I'd get upset at him if he was working late, he wouldn't explain why he needed to stay at work, and we'd bottle it up. Instead of talking about things, we kept it inside until it grew and grew and became something ugly inside of us. Does that make sense?" She stopped and gently touched my hand. Boy, did I understand what that was like.

"It seems like lately my special talent is hiding my feelings," I told the two of them, because if they were being honest, so could I.

Mom nodded and continued. "We started to resent each other, but the thing was, when you don't speak about what's bothering you, the other person doesn't know what's wrong.

That was us. We expected the other person to know why we were so mad, and that wasn't fair."

"We needed to talk to each other, but instead, we tried to avoid our issues until they grew way too big for us to handle," Dad said. "And while sometimes a break is a good idea, the reason we did it might not have been. We were running away from things instead of facing them head-on, and in the process, our family got hurt."

"It felt like you were running from Claire and me," I told Dad. I picked up a big piece of pancake and dragged it across the syrup on my plate before popping it into my mouth.

"And that's the worst part. I made you feel that way. I missed out on some very important things in your life," he said, and he looked so sad. Not like a person who would ditch his kids at all but like someone who missed his kids. "Running away from you and Claire is the last thing I'd ever do. I love you two so much."

I believed him, and I kind of got what they were saying about what happened between the two of them. It wasn't much different from the way I'd been acting lately. I hadn't been honest with a lot of people. Look at how everything blew up in my face with the secrets I asked Mom and Dad to keep from each other. And with Evan. I liked him, but I was too chicken to say anything about it. And with Lizzie. At what point does a life full of half-truths become more real than one where you're honest with yourself and others? I wasn't quite sure, but I was scared I was heading that way.

"Sometimes," I said to Mom and Dad slowly, "it's scary to be honest, because it's easier to keep things to yourself or lie."

Mom reached out and put her hand over mine. "You're a wise girl, Grace. But it all comes back to you, whether or not you want it there. And we need to be strong and make sure we're not fooling ourselves."

"But how do I know I won't get hurt?" I asked my parents.

"You don't," Mom said. "Just like Dad and I don't know what the future holds. But you better believe we're going to try as hard as we can."

CHAPTER
Thirty-Eight

AFTER WE STUFFED OURSELVES ON PAN-
cakes and Dad drove me to school, I waved good-bye and
walked toward the building, but then thought better of it,
turned, and ran over to the driver's-side door. I gestured at
him to roll down his window.

"Did you forget something?"

I stood on my tiptoes and leaned into the car. I wrapped
my arms around him and tried to hug him through the window. I smiled as I pulled back. "Nope, I just wanted to tell you
that I love you."

Dad reached out and grabbed my hand. He gave it a tight
squeeze. "I love you too, kiddo."

I waved one more time and headed into the school, not caring who saw me hug Dad, because he was my dad and he was back and that was pretty great.

"So I wanted to talk to you," I said to Lizzie when I found her by her locker.

"Don't worry, I heard you on the walkie-talkie last night. We don't need to do Operation Pucker Up anymore," she said, and paused to tie her shoe even though it wasn't unlaced.

"Really?" I asked. This was not like Lizzie at all. "You're going to stop without a fight?"

Lizzie shrugged, but I wasn't convinced. Something was up. She couldn't even look me in the eye, and she loved Operation Pucker Up.

"What's going on?" I asked, and eyed her suspiciously.

"Don't be mad at me," she said, and bit her bottom lip. "I lost the notebook. It was at rehearsal yesterday, I know it was, because I wrote in it between scenes. But after I came back from running through the opening number with everyone, it was gone. I dumped out everything in my bag in case I shoved it in there, but it was missing."

I felt the world around me spin. It reminded me of all those times when we spun around and around and tried to run but couldn't stay up straight. We moved forward, slanted and dizzy, until we fell to the grass in fits of laughter. Right now I had the same feeling, but I sure wasn't laughing.

"Please don't hate me," Lizzie said. Her hand went to the yellow ribbon in her hair and she twirled it around her fingers. "I searched everywhere. I even came here early this morning and walked around the rehearsal room. I don't know what happened to it."

"Someone took it." I knew exactly who would steal a notebook. It was no secret that we were doing something with it. We carried it around everywhere and made it very obvious that the notebook was important. I let out a long, mournful groan. "All that stuff inside. Oh my gosh."

I felt a second wave of dizziness when I thought about the lists, detailed outlines, and notes Lizzie kept in the notebook. Anyone with half a brain would totally understand what was going on once they read the pages.

"I'm so sorry, Grace. Really, I am."

I held up my hand to get her to stop. It was all I could do, because I didn't have the right words to tell her how truly awful this was.

CHAPTER
Thirty-Nine

"ANYONE CAN BE A SUSPECT," BECK WHIS-
pered, and I half expected him to be wearing a tweed cap and
holding a big magnifying glass like some old-time detective.
The three of us sat in the third row of seats in the theater waiting for Mrs. Hiser to come out and give us her notes about the
run-through we just did. Beck was plotting his mission to get
back the notebook, while I kept waiting to see someone up
onstage waving it high, ready to do a theatrical reading from it.

"Anyone? So, do you think Mr. Westmeyer took our notebook?" I said, pointing at our school's custodian, a man so old
he was probably custodian when my great-grandpa went to
school here.

Mr. Westmeyer moved slowly down the aisle, checking the seats for pieces of garbage. I swear I could hear his bones creaking.

"Okay, maybe not him," Beck agreed. "But you can't rule out any potential suspects."

"I don't have suspects, because I know who took it." I tilted my head toward Michelle, who caught me looking at her. She gave me a little wave with her fingers and smirked.

"She so has it," Lizzie said, and narrowed her eyes at Michelle. "And I want it back."

"She's probably showed it to a bunch of people by now." I put my head in my hands.

"She'll be sorry if she did." Lizzie cracked her knuckles as if she was about to get in a fight. I cringed, but I wouldn't have been surprised if Lizzie had jumped out of her seat and gone after Michelle. Luckily, Mrs. Hiser interrupted. What happens during the final rehearsals before the show is that after each run-through, we gather together and Mrs. Hiser tells us what worked and didn't work in the show. Well, mostly what didn't work, but she always throws in some positives so we don't feel like complete failures. I watched Michelle and got more and more mad as Mrs. Hiser gave everyone her notes.

"Now go home and get some rest," Mrs. Hiser told us when she finished. "We open in a week, and I need you to be in good shape for our final rehearsals."

Michelle turned around in her seat, caught my eye, and slowly raised her hand. "Mrs. Hiser, we've run through the play a few times, but we keep skipping over the part where the prince wakes Snow White up. Shouldn't we practice everything? I mean, what if something goes wrong?"

I clenched my teeth and tried not to appear upset. I wanted to show her what could go wrong, but I'm a lover and not a fighter, so that's why I sat silently plotting different forms of revenge in my head. It was as if everyone was watching a game of Ping-Pong as they turned from James to me, back and forth, back and forth. There was a hum in the theater as the cast waited for Mrs. Hiser's reply.

"Thank you for your concern, Michelle," she said, trying to settle everyone down. "I can assure you that Grace and James will be ready for the scene come opening night."

I didn't dare look at James when I got up to leave. I ran up the aisle steps so fast, I almost tripped and fell flat on my face. I stopped for a moment at the top to catch my breath, and Michelle took that as her opportunity to swoop in and continue to make her role as the Evil Queen reflect her real life.

 221

"Is the widdle Grace nervous about her big kiss?" she whispered in my ear, using baby talk. She opened her bag wide enough so that I could see the cover of Lizzie's notebook. "Maybe you should ask your mommy to wead you a bedtime story so you know what to do."

Beck and Lizzie came up from behind. Michelle scowled at Lizzie and zipped up her bag, hurrying out of the theater before I could fill Lizzie and Beck in on what just happened.

"She has the notebook," I said. "I saw it."

"Let's go get her!" Lizzie shouted, and moved to follow Michelle. I grabbed the bottom of her shirt and pulled her back to me.

"No, forget it. This has gone too far. I don't want to start a war. I told you last night I was done with Operation Pucker Up, and I meant it. It's time to come clean." I took a deep breath. "I'm going to talk to James and tell him the truth before Michelle shows him the notebook."

Lizzie stared at me like I was crazy, but Beck slapped me on the back. "Good luck, Grace. You're a brave girl."

But the thing was, I wasn't. I was a coward, and I had been for a long time. I'd been hiding behind my friends and this plan, instead of being truthful. With everyone. I was done trying to pretend I was an expert on things I knew nothing about. It was time to fess up, even if it made me look like a fool, because the truth was, everything I had done in the past few months had made me look like a fool. What did I have to lose? It was what I had to gain that made me walk back down the aisle and approach James.

CHAPTER
Forty

OKAY, SO I'LL ADMIT I ONLY HELD ON TO that courage for about ten seconds. After that, my whole body was telling me to run, run, run. But I fought the feeling and made my way to James. He was standing with a bunch of other kids from the play, and they were all laughing about a joke one of them had made.

I thought about how Mom said that when people kept things inside, it could sometimes do more harm than good. If we don't share what worries or upsets us, how can we ever expect someone to understand us? It felt so good that afternoon with Evan, when we yelled all those things on the bridge with the train below us, and when I told Lizzie I was upset that she wouldn't listen to me talk about Dad. I needed to share my secret with James.

"Hey, Grace," he said when I tapped him on the shoulder. "Are you ready for opening night?"

"I think so," I said. "As long as I don't forget any of my lines."

"You're doing great. You'll be fine."

"Thanks," I said, and thought over how much I'd stressed about this play and the kiss at the end. It was time to stop those feelings. "Can I talk to you? Alone?"

James looked surprised, and I didn't blame him. I'd spent more time hiding from him or turning red when he came near than actually talking with him. He nodded, though, and picked up his book bag. We walked out together. I led the way and didn't stop until we reached the playground on the other side of the school. I sat down on a swing and he did the same.

"What's up?" he asked as he twisted his swing around tight and then let it go, twirling back the other way. Dust kicked up all over him.

"It's about the play," I said. I pumped my feet until I was moving back and forth, higher and higher. "About the end of the play."

"The end?" James asked. He didn't get it.

"When you wake me up," I told him, and swung so high I was afraid I was going to flip over. I didn't care, though; it was easier than staying on the ground and talking directly to James. "The thing is . . . I'm really nervous about it."

I whooshed back down and tipped my head back, feeling my hair brush against the ground before I went back up.

"I'm nervous about it too," James said.

I slowed a little. "You are?"

"Yeah, sure, it's kind of a big deal. There's going to be a lot of people there."

"Tell me about it." I stopped my swing so I was even with James. The two of us hung side by side. "But I'm not nervous about the people. I'm nervous about the kiss. I've never kissed anyone before."

He didn't say anything, and my stomach sank. He was staring at me with his eyebrows slightly raised. He looked as if he was trying not to laugh, and I waited for it, my whole body tense.

"Forget it," I said, jumping up. "This was stupid. I shouldn't have said anything."

I stomped away, hating myself for being such a dummy.

"Wait, Grace, stop."

"No," I yelled over my shoulder.

 226

"It's okay," James said, trying to get me to stop again. "I haven't kissed anyone either."

I stopped. *James has never kissed anyone before?*

I swung around, my hands on my hips. "You're just trying to make me feel better." I scowled at him. I bet Michelle had already told him about Operation Pucker Up and he was about to make a big fool out of me.

"I wish I was," James said, and smiled sheepishly. "But we're in the same boat. I've never kissed a girl."

"For real?"

"I swear on my LeBron James autographed basketball, and that thing is worth a lot of money."

He was telling the truth. No one would swear on something so important.

"So this kiss thing has been stressing you out too, huh?" James asked.

"If you only knew," I told him, and laughed. It wasn't even funny, but after the first few laughs came out, I couldn't stop, and soon my whole body was shaking and I couldn't catch my breath. James eyed me as if I was a lunatic at first, but then he joined in. The two of us, doubled over on the grass, were cracking up about the fact that neither of us knew quite what to do. And I was 100 percent okay with that.

I told James everything. I figured I might as well, because if I didn't, Michelle would. He promised to talk with her and deal with the notebook if I promised to keep quiet about the no-kissing thing. I made a cross over my heart and told him his secret was safe with me. I didn't want to ruin his rock star/leading man image.

I walked home, turning over what James told me in my mind. I couldn't believe he hadn't kissed anyone yet and that he was just like me. Could I have this kissing thing all wrong? Maybe there were tons of us walking around the school, thinking our lives were over because we hadn't had our first kisses, when in reality we were all rushing toward something only a few people had done at our age. After all, Mom didn't kiss Dad until her sophomore year in high school, and I knew Lizzie and Beck still hadn't kissed anyone. Maybe this big deal wasn't such a big deal after all.

CHAPTER
Forty-One

I WAS ON PINS AND NEEDLES AS I WAITED for Michelle to do something horrible and awful with the notebook. After all, she was the Evil Queen and did a great job already living up to her role. I envisioned her making copies of the pages and plastering the school with them, or getting up onstage and doing a dramatic reading of all our ideas.

I was also trying to forget that Evan existed. My parents only let me out to go to rehearsals and watched me at home to make sure I couldn't sneak off, which was fine with me. There was no way I wanted to step out of the house and risk running into Evan.

My parents, on the other hand, were a little harder to avoid, but I no longer felt like Dad didn't belong in the house. They were both trying to be more truthful, and that made things easier. They even told me they were going to marriage counseling and wanted to have a weekly date night if I didn't mind babysitting Claire.

Rehearsals flew by, and suddenly we were two days to opening night.

I was talking with James backstage about one of the scenes where the dwarfs and I had to get offstage and he had to get onstage. We couldn't seem to do the switch quickly enough, and we all ended up running into one another.

"What if you all froze in place until I got out there, and then once I did, you could all move offstage?" he offered.

"That could work," I told him, hoping we had figured out a way to avoid a collision.

"Well, well, well . . . ," Michelle said, sneaking up behind us. "What are you two talking so seriously about?"

"We're kind of busy right now. Do you need us for anything?" James asked, while my stomach dipped. I had a feeling Michelle was up to no good.

"Oh, it's nothing too important. I just wanted to ask you how Operation Pucker Up was going." She smiled at me with a sickly sweet smile. Here it was, the bomb I had been waiting for her to drop, and of course it would only make sense for her to do it in front of James so she could make sure that I was thoroughly embarrassed.

"What's Operation Pucker Up?" James asked, and I wished for a poison apple so I could fall into a deep, deep sleep and not have to deal with any of this.

"Nothing—" I said at the same time Michelle spoke.

"Oh, just a little plan that Grace and her friends concocted so she could get her first kiss. Seems like she was nervous about having to kiss you at the end of the play. Just like I said. She's an amateur. She can't hack it onstage. That role should have been mine."

I waited for James to start laughing, but he didn't do that. Instead, he faced Michelle head-on, and he looked angry.

"Really?" he asked her. "You're going to give Grace a hard time about kissing someone onstage? Weren't you the one who was nervous about dancing with Colin two years ago in *Cinderella*? You asked Mrs. Hiser if the two of you could say your lines at the punch bowl instead of waltzing."

"You were afraid to dance with a boy?" I asked, trying not to giggle.

Michelle scowled at the two of us. "I wasn't afraid, I just

thought it would make more sense if we were standing still when we talked."

"Was that before or after you tripped during rehearsal and knocked down one of the set pieces?" James asked, and I had never been more grateful.

"Whatever," Michelle said, getting upset. "At least I didn't make a list to try to kiss someone."

"It's called research," I shot back. "And if you don't mind, right now James and I are trying to research our roles. But I guess that's what you're doing too, right? Practicing being evil?"

Michelle's mouth opened and closed as she tried to come up with a comeback, and finally she just threw her hands up in the air. "Forget it. I don't have time for the two of you."

She turned and stomped away.

"Did she really knock down a piece of the set when she was dancing?" I asked James with a smile.

"Yep, one of the columns in the ballroom crashed to the ground. Let's just say that opening night wasn't the only thing that was a smash hit during that play."

I laughed so loud that I snorted, but I didn't care. I was glad that I had told James the truth about not kissing someone, because when you let go of the things that were worrying you, nothing can bother you. Not even Michelle.

CHAPTER
Forty-Two

I WOKE UP TO SUNLIGHT STREAMING through the window and took it as a sign that opening night was going to be great. Mrs. Hiser stayed true to her word and didn't make us practice the kiss, which was both a blessing and a curse. There is something to be said about having courage when the event is still in the future. When it is right in front of you, the definition of courage becomes a different story.

I stared at the ceiling and tried to brainstorm alternatives to the kiss. Maybe I could turn my head when James went for the kiss? Or let out a big snore? I could tell him to pretend to kiss me, but our lips wouldn't touch. Or I could wake up by myself. I could rewrite the ending so the apple's powers wore off me. I laughed to myself, thinking about what James would do if I opened my eyes before he kissed me. It calmed me a bit, but I knew that wasn't an option. Everyone had worked too hard for me to mess it up.

I sat in my room, cross-legged on the bed. I wore my cast sweatshirt, with our names and parts printed on the back, which was a tradition at school. Everyone wore these shirts all day to promote opening night.

I held my walkie-talkie in my hands and turned it over and over. Even though I'd never admit it to anyone, I was tired of being mad. I missed talking with Evan when we ran into each other outside.

I turned it on to see what would happen. I pressed the red button on the side.

"Hello?" I said, more a question than anything else.

I waited but got nothing back.

"Anyone there?" I asked, not quite sure what I was doing. Or, at least, I wasn't going to admit what I was doing. Not even to myself.

I held it up to the window, as if Evan could see it, even though it was silly.

Someone knocked on my door, and I shoved my walkie-talkie under my pillow.

 234

"Come in," I said.

"Mind if we talk?" Dad asked as he stuck his head in the door with the same sad smile that made me feel awful because part of it was my fault. It didn't seem right that my own dad should be hesitant about stepping into my room, but try as I might, it was so hard to let go of all my hurt. Or, more important, to let go of my fear.

"Sure," I said. He came in, pulled out my desk chair, and sat down. His eyes went to the picture I had pulled out a while ago. It was of the two of us after opening night of *Annie*. I was one of the orphans, and Dad's hand was slung over my shoulder, the two of us laughing at the camera. I remember exactly what made us laugh: Dad told me a lame Daddy Warbucks joke about the glare on his bald head blinding everyone. I thought about how excited I was for him to see me in that show and how, despite everything that had happened between then and now, I was glad he would see me tonight as Snow White.

"I wanted to tell you how proud I am of you," he said. "Not only as an actress, but as my daughter. You've dealt with a lot this year, and you've been so brave and kind to Claire and your mother. I couldn't have asked for a daughter more incredible than you."

"I needed to be strong," I told him, but it made me feel good that he noticed. "What else could I have done?"

"You've taught me a lot, Grace."

"What do you mean?" I asked. I taught Dad? What could a kid teach her father?

"You face things head-on. You're fearless, and that's an amazing thing to be."

"I've never thought of myself as brave before," I said.

"You are. I see it in you every day, and so does Claire. That's why she looks up to you so much. We could all learn a thing or two from you."

I looked at Dad skeptically, but maybe he was right. Maybe it was time to think of myself as brave.

"I usually give you flowers," Dad said, reaching into his back pocket, "but it seems to me that tonight's show is a little more special than a bouquet of flowers that would last for only a few days."

He handed me a box wrapped in red paper, the same color as the big shiny apples I had been biting into during rehearsal the past few weeks.

I opened it slowly, revealing a box under the paper. When I took the lid off, I gasped. Inside was a silver bracelet with a little apple charm hanging from it.

 236

"I thought we could work together to add to that. A charm for each play you're in from now on."

"That might be a lot of charms," I said, laughing. "I don't plan on stopping anytime soon. Tonight, Sloane Middle School; tomorrow, Broadway!"

"And I plan to be at each and every opening night. Even when I'm old and gray and have to hobble there with my cane."

"I'll make sure you get the senior citizen discount," I joked.

Dad laughed a deep belly laugh that shook his whole body, but then he turned serious. "I know I've hurt you, Grace. But that's in the past. I'm here for good now, and you can't get rid of me if you try. And this is a tradition that I don't plan to ever stop."

"Ever?" I asked, thinking about the last play he missed.

"Never," Dad said, and I knew we weren't just talking about my shows. I allowed my fear to evaporate and let myself trust him, because without trust, what did I have?

Forty-Three

THERE IS NOTHING LIKE OPENING NIGHT in the theater. It's almost always a guaranteed full house, the energy is electric, and the cast is ready to show everybody what they've got. Tonight was no exception, even if I was simultaneously battling butterflies in my stomach and the urge to jump around and shout "Yippee!"

"Are you ready for this?" Beck asked, rosy cheeks painted on because apparently that's what makes a dwarf in our school's version of *Snow White*. All seven of them had bright red cheeks. The first time I saw them walk out onto the stage, I laughed so hard that Mrs. Hiser stopped the dress rehearsal until I calmed down.

Operation Pucker Up

"As ready as I'll ever be," I said, and grinned. I was dressed in my blue and yellow dress, exactly like the Disney version. There was a pocket on the side, so I slipped Dad's bracelet and my marble in it for good luck. My black hair was curled under and sprayed so much, I could walk through a hurricane and it would still be perfect.

Beck and I peeked out of a separation in the curtains and watched the theater fill with people. I spotted my parents and Claire, who carried a giant bouquet and kept knocking it into the man in front of her as they walked down to their seats, seven rows back from the stage, the perfect distance we discovered after years of watching shows.

"Hey, are you two ready to break some legs?" Lizzie asked, coming up behind us. It was bad luck in the theater to wish someone luck before a show; instead, you told them to break a leg, which always made me more nervous. Breaking a leg was the last thing that I wanted to do.

Lizzie was in her ensemble costume, a pale peach dress with her hair on top of her head in two braids. She insisted on her trademark ribbon, so a white satin one was wrapped around the braids. Her lipstick was a pale, shimmery pink, the opposite of my bright red color to give me lips as red as blood.

"I sure hope so," I said, and my stomach flip-flopped. I

couldn't believe I'd be out onstage in less than half an hour.

"I have an opening-night gift for you," Lizzie said, and shoved a bag at me.

"A gift? I didn't get you anything," I said, feeling slightly embarrassed. Lizzie was way too nice sometimes.

"I don't need a gift. This is a special one just for you. Open it," she said as she jumped from foot to foot in excitement. Whatever was in the bag, she couldn't wait for me to see.

I reached in and pulled out a book.

Wait.

Not just any book. The Operation Pucker Up notebook!

"How did you get this?" I asked, so glad it was now in my possession, especially after Michelle had tried to tell James about it. Who knows what other plans she might have been concocting to embarrass me?

"Michelle needs to be more careful about leaving her bag sitting out. I grabbed it when she was getting her makeup done by one of the parent volunteers." Lizzie put her palms out and shrugged. "That girl is so careless sometimes. And it appears she's in need of a little help from our expert skills."

"Expert skills?" I raised an eyebrow in disbelief. "I'd hardly call us experts."

"Say what you will, but Michelle is a fan of some of our ideas." Lizzie opened the book, and sure enough, the corners were turned down on a few pages. Michelle even went so far as to highlight one of the items on the list: *Wear plenty of perfume, guys love girls who smell sweet.*

"You're kidding me," I said, and cracked up. "Michelle is a fan of Operation Pucker Up?"

"I bet if we passed her right now, she'd smell pretty good," Lizzie added, and laughed. The two of us tried to stop and catch our breath, but each time we did, one of us would start up again and we'd laugh so hard we snorted.

"So you're going to go for it?" Lizzie asked. She straightened the red satin bow tied in my hair and stepped back to inspect me.

"What happens, happens," I told her. "There's no use worrying about these things."

That wasn't exactly true, but true enough to stop Lizzie from bugging me about the kiss.

"I think you'll do great," Beck said. "Even if I messed up the practice kiss."

I held the palm of my hand up to stop him. "I thought we agreed to never talk about that again."

"Talk about what?" Beck asked.

I grinned, so glad to have friends like Beck and Lizzie.

James walked past with a bunch of his friends, and the nervous feeling returned. I pulled back a part of the curtain again to distract myself, and the three of us huddled together and tried to peek out without the people in the audience catching us. Lizzie was in the middle and slung an arm around each of us. It had been a long road to get to this point, but I was glad I was able to do it with Beck and Lizzie. We stood there, taking it all in, until the lights in the theater flashed, signaling to the audience that it was time to take their seats.

"Ten minutes until showtime," one of the stage managers said, an eighth grader who snapped at us if we were too loud backstage. We tiptoed past him, not wanting the wrath of his anger before the show.

"I need to finish getting ready," Beck said. He gave me a hug and whispered in my ear, "You're a star, you're going to wow them tonight."

"Thanks." I hoped he was right.

"Go get 'em, girl," Lizzie said, and waved good-bye as she took her spot onstage with the rest of the townspeople for the opening scene.

I stepped back into the wings. I had ten minutes before the Evil Queen gazed into her magic mirror and I stepped onto the stage. I was ready to go, and it was more fun to watch what was going on onstage than get all nervous waiting in the greenroom.

The lights went down, the audience got quiet, and the curtain rose. The show had begun. And as the lights went back up on the stage, someone grabbed my hand.

CHAPTER
Forty-Four

"I NEED TO TALK TO YOU," EVAN SAID. "Please don't run away."

I gasped, which resulted in a dirty look from the cranky stagehand. I shook myself out of Evan's grip and pulled him into a back corner. The prop corner. The same place I'd made a fool out of myself with Beck. But it was the only place I could think of that was empty right now, yet still close enough to the stage that I wouldn't miss my cue.

"What are you doing here? How did you get backstage?" I asked.

"I snuck in through the side door. I think everyone thought I was part of the crew; I dressed the part." He gestured to his outfit. He wore black, from his black tennis shoes to the tip of his black knitted hat.

"I needed to talk to you before the show," he said. "I didn't know how else to get to you, since you made it very clear that you were avoiding me at home."

"I had a good reason to stay away from you," I told him, my hands on my hips. "What you did was awful. You listened to my private conversations with Lizzie."

"I didn't do it to be mean." He paused and shook his hair out of his eyes. "I . . . uh . . . did it because I liked you. It was wrong, but I couldn't stop."

Wait.

Evan liked me?

"But you know all my secrets," I said. "Everything I worried about, the stupid plans we made."

"And I hated that you were upset about so many things. I wanted to help, but I didn't know how."

"It's so embarrassing, thinking of you knowing all my private thoughts."

"I'll never repeat any of it." Evan looked so sorry that I couldn't help but believe him.

I glanced down at my costume and remembered where I was. "You came to my play."

"You told me I could, so I hoped the offer was still there."

"I said you couldn't come to opening night."

He stuck his hands in his back pocket and shifted his weight. "But I have a good reason to come tonight. There's something I want to do before it's too late."

"What?" I whispered, my heart doing a crazy pounding dance in my chest.

"Kiss you," he said quietly.

I nodded my head slightly and wondered how I was still standing when it felt like I was whooshing down a giant hill on a roller coaster. My hands were super sweaty, and I wiped them on the sides of my dress.

Evan took a step toward me until we were so close that I could smell his cinnamon gum.

Slowly, slowly, his lips met mine, and it was wonderful and amazing and quite possibly the best thing to ever happen to me. My lips tingled when we separated and then the audience broke into applause.

We jumped apart and turned toward the stage at the same time. I knew it was impossible, but I was scared that somehow the curtains had opened wide, even the back scrim, and the entire theater had watched my first kiss.

I let out a sigh of relief when I realized what was really

happening. "They're only clapping because it's the end of the scene," I said, and Evan relaxed.

"Phew. Thank goodness," he said, and I couldn't agree more.

"I better go," I said, even though I kind of wanted to stay there all night long. "It's almost my cue."

"Can I see you after the show?" he asked.

"Of course, but you might need to fight your way through my adoring fans," I joked.

"If I can't make it through to you, there's always the walkie-talkies," Evan said, and I groaned.

"You're nuts if you think I'm talking with Lizzie on those again," I said. But it might be fun to talk with Evan on them.

We both stood there grinning like two idiots until Lizzie found us. She froze when she saw the two of us together and tilted her head, as if inspecting what was in front of her. She squinted her eyes, and I felt uncomfortable.

"You need to get moving, Snow White," she finally said. "Your big moment is about to begin."

I let her push me away from Evan, and as I stepped out under the hot lights, I thought about how Lizzie was wrong. My big moment had already happened, and it had involved a boy named Evan.

CHAPTER
Forty-Five

THINGS WENT OFF WITHOUT A HITCH AT the end of the show. When James bent down to kiss me, I didn't sneeze, laugh, or do any other embarrassing thing that I'd never be able to live down. In fact, it was all very uneventful and, the truth was, . . . kind of boring. I mean, come on, after kissing Evan, the stage kiss with James didn't even stand a chance.

Beck claimed James looked terrified as he bent down to kiss me, but since my eyes were closed, I'll never know. I woke up, the audience cheered, and it was pretty incredible.

But the best part of it all was after the show.

We were allowed to go out into the audience in our costumes. Even though Mrs. Hiser told us real actors wouldn't, because it would break the magic of the illusion, we begged her to let us do it tonight. We wanted to show off and get lots of pictures to remember this moment. I hurried out the side door and made my way through the packed crowd, searching for someone in particular. People stopped me to say congratulations, and I smiled and thanked them and moved on.

I finally found him, off to the side by the ticket booth. He was leaning against the wall, staring out into the crowd, and when I caught his eye, his whole face broke into a smile.

I didn't care about all the other people around me; I ran toward Dad.

I ran toward my entire family, and when I reached them, I threw my arms around all three in a big group hug, because this was the way it was supposed to be.

We were together, and maybe the future would be hard and we might not live happily ever after right away, but for this moment, at this one place, we were a family again, and that's all that mattered.

Acknowledgments

WRITING A BOOK IS A LOT LIKE PUTTING on a production of a play. Each involves a huge cast of characters and backstage crew. So I'd like to ask for a round of applause for the following people.

Thank you to my wonderful agent, Natalie Lakosil, who has cheered on *Operation Pucker Up* from the start and found the perfect home for it. Thank you to my editor, Alyson Heller, for loving Grace as much as I do (not to mention for loving musicals and gummy candy as much as I do too!), and to everyone on the Aladdin M!X team, who worked so hard on *Operation Pucker Up* (including a big shout-out to Frank Montagna for designing the cutest cover in the world!).

A million thanks to Nova Ren Suma and the Thursday Girls, especially to my Writing Soul Sister, Elle LaMarca, for all your encouragement and cheering while I wrote this book (one day I'll thank you in person!). And a huge thanks to my early readers, who read some or all of this book: Leigh Stavar, Lee Bross, Nancy Skinner, Lindsey Scheibe, Corey Haydu, Jennifer Mann, Kari Olsen, and Taryn Albright.

My husband and family are the best and have encouraged my writing from the beginning. And I can't thank the students and staff at Perry High School enough for being some of my biggest fans. You all rock!

I'd like to give a standing ovation to those people who had leading roles in my life during middle school and high school, when much of my time was spent at Lakewood Little Theater. I owe so much to some of the most talented people I know, the Beck Center crew. In particular, thank you to Betsy Kahl, Rory O'Malley, Nick Lowe, Jim Asmus, Michelle Cichra, Katie Conway, Adam Moeller, and Bobby Moran. My life is so much better for knowing all of you. What would I have done without Saturday morning classes, walks to McDonald's, basement hangouts, *The Princess Bride*, Odar, and cheese? Who ever thought some of my greatest memories would involve my wearing a bunny costume or dancing onstage with Slinkys in my hair?! I couldn't have asked for better friends, and this book is for all of you.